SOLOING OVER CHANGES

JODY FISHER

**THE ULTIMATE GUIDE TO IMPROVISING
WITH SCALES OVER CHORDS ON THE GUITAR**

The accompanying audio for this book is available
to stream or download online. For free access, visit:
www.alfred.com/redeem

Enter the unique code found on the inside cover.

Alfred Music
P.O. Box 10003
Van Nuys, CA 91410-0003
alfred.com

ISBN-10: 1-4706-2764-7 (Book & Online Audio)
ISBN-13: 978-1-4706-2764-5 (Book & Online Audio)

Cover Photos : Front cover guitarist: © iStockphoto.com / Driftwood • Author photo courtesy of Jody Fisher

 Alfred Cares. Contents printed on environmentally responsible paper.

CONTENTS

 This symbol indicates that the example it is next to is on the recording. The track number below the symbol corresponds directly to the example you want to hear. Track 1 will help you tune your guitar to the recording.

ABOUT THE AUTHOR

Jody Fisher has been playing and teaching guitar professionally since the early 1970s. On stage, he has performed in almost every style of music—from rock and pop to jazz and original music—and has toured extensively in the United States, Canada, Europe, and Asia.

As an educator, Jody has taught for decades at numerous university-level institutions, including the University of Redlands, the University of La Verne, Los Angeles Music Academy (also known as Los Angeles College of Music), Riverside Community College, Jazz Education Abroad (JEA), and the National Guitar Workshop, where he served as an associate director and clinician for over 20 years.

Jody is also a notable author who has written many books for Alfred Music. For more information, go to www.jodyfisher.com.

INTRODUCTION

Every musician uses and practices scales. For some, scales are used as exercises to promote speed and dexterity. For others, they are a course of study to understand the relationship between chords, arpeggios, and melodies. For most guitarists, working on scales is a way to improve their ability to improvise, regardless of the style of music they play.

Most guitarists begin improvising with major and minor pentatonic scales exclusively, and these scales sound great over most blues and rock chord progressions. When we start to learn about scales used in other kinds of music, we might assume that improvising with those new scales will follow the same routine. But, using scales to improvise is only part of the story. In reality, many other tools are used along with scales. Improvisers must also study concepts like vocabulary (or licks), arpeggios, chord substitution, contour, and many others. Of course, we all hope for moments of brilliant, spontaneous ideas to occur—and they will if the player has studied well.

Scales do play a very important part in all of this, but most players have never been taught how to learn, practice, or get the most out of the scales they use. Hopefully, this book will fill that need.

Book Organization

This book is organized into two parts. Part 1, pages 6–48, covers the initial process of learning a scale and practicing it, including the various ways to work with a scale to create melodies for your improvisations. This will help you get the most out of using scales. What you learn here is applicable to all styles of music.

Most of Part 1 uses the major scale exclusively, and only one fingering will be used for each example. This will enable you to easily compare the various techniques you are working on. After you gain some experience with these techniques, apply them to other fingerings for the major scale as well (make sure you know five or six fingerings for the major scale). Once you have done this, you will want to use these same techniques for other scales you learn in the future. This should be a regular routine whenever you decide to learn any new scale.

Part 2, which begins on page 49, is a comprehensive reference guide for choosing what scales to use over what chords—with both chords and scales clearly highlighted. It has a cross-referenced table of contents so you can either look up a chord and learn what scale to use over it, or look up a scale and learn what chords it will work with.

Before trying to learn more exotic scales, make sure you know a few different fingerings for each scale listed at the bottom of page 48, as those are the most essential for most musicians. By working slowly and accurately, you will find real improvement and greater expression in your improvised soloing.

How to Use This Book

This book is intended for guitarists of all styles past the earliest beginning levels (advanced beginners and above). If you are relatively new to playing and improvising with scales, start at the very beginning of Chapter 1 to make sure you understand each concept before moving on to the next idea. To gain the most from this book, you should already have some experience playing the guitar and have a solid understanding of music fundamentals (how to read music and TAB, including accidentals, key signatures, etc.). Guitar fundamentals like basic picking and strumming, making chords and changing them, and tuning should come easily and be natural for you. If these areas are difficult for you, you should probably get help from a good teacher. The stronger your grasp of the fundamentals, the more easily you will absorb the ideas in this book.

If you are an intermediate player with some experience using scales for improvising in blues and rock styles, it is suggested that you go through the chapters on learning, practicing, and working with scales (Chapters 2–5) to see if there are any ideas that you might not have picked up yet. If you find gaps in your knowledge, stop and work on those ideas before moving on.

If you are a more experienced player and are familiar with all the techniques shown in this book, then go to page 48 to find the most important scales to know. If any are missing from your vocabulary, start there and be sure you know multiple fingerings for each scale and can play them in every key easily. At that point, you will enjoy learning, exploring, and applying some new scales from the extensive information in Part 2 that starts on page 49.

PART 1: LEARNING AND USING SCALES

CHAPTER 1

What Is a Scale?

A *scale* is a set of tones in a specific order of intervals that generally represent a particular tonality from which we can compose (or improvise) melodies. By combining these tones in various ways, we can create chords to accompany these melodies, or create melodies that sound good over the chords. Once you understand the relationship between the notes of a scale and the chords that exist within the scale, you will gain a lot more control over your improvised solos and compositions.

If you are new to working with scales, there are a few preliminary concepts you should understand. Let's begin with intervals.

Intervals

An *interval* in music is generally defined as the distance between two notes. There are actually two names (or labels) we use to describe an interval: a numeric name and a quality name. The numeric name involves the alphabetical distance from one note to another. For instance, the distance from the note C to E is called a 3rd, because we would count C–D–E, the distance of three notes, to go from C to E. (The note we start from is included in the count.) So, the interval from C to F is a 4th, C to G is a 5th, and so on.

The quality of an interval is determined by the number of half steps between the notes. For instance, the distance from C to E is four half steps and is called a *major* 3rd, while the distance from C to E♭ is three half steps and is called a *minor* 3rd. The distance from C to A is nine half steps and is described as a major 6th, while the distance between C to A♭ is eight half steps and is called a minor 6th. Below is a breakdown of the types of interval quality names we use:

- The terms major or minor are used for these intervals: 2nds, 3rds, 6ths, 7ths, 9ths, and 13ths.

- The term *perfect* is used for these intervals: unisons, 4ths (the 11th, which is the same note, shows up in chords), 5ths, and octaves

- The terms *diminished* and *augmented* generally apply to altered intervals of 4ths and 5ths. (Note: the terms "lowered" and "raised" are sometimes used instead of diminished and augmented.)

The chart below shows most of the common intervals you should be familiar with.

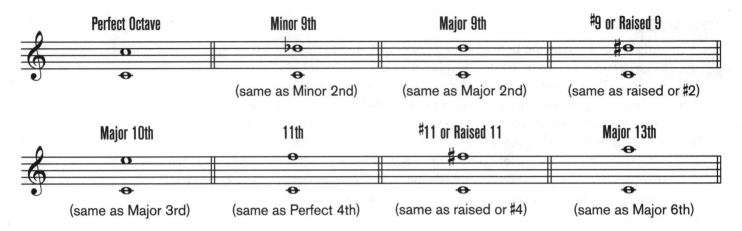

Intervals can be either ascending or descending. This chart shows both directions from the note C.

Interval Inversion

To *invert* an interval, take the bottom note and bump it up one octave, or take the top note and move it down one octave. This will create a different interval, and it's an important concept to grasp because it helps with understanding the nature of note relationships and aids in communicating with other musicians. For instance, you might be asked to transpose a phrase (or an entire song) up a minor 7th. If you were familiar with inverting intervals, you could approach the transposition by going down a major 2nd instead and know you'll arrive at the same place. Obviously, it's easier to go down a major 2nd, which is only two frets away on a guitar, than to try to transpose all your fingerings up a minor 7th, which would probably require you to find a whole new way to play the song (or phrase).

The rules for inverting intervals are easy to remember. After inverting, a:

- Major interval becomes minor
- Minor interval becomes major
- Perfect interval remains perfect
- Diminished interval becomes augmented, and an augmented interval becomes diminished

Numerically, the sum of the two intervals will always equal nine. For example, a major 3rd becomes a minor 6th (3 + 6 = 9), a minor 2nd becomes a major 7th, a perfect 5th becomes a perfect 4th, an augmented 4th becomes a diminished 5th, and so on. All of the preceding pairs of inverted intervals add up to nine.

Check out these examples:

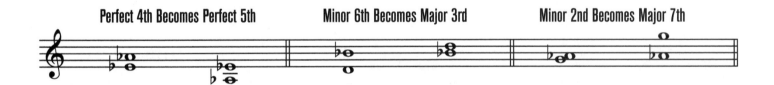

The Chromatic Scale

The most basic concept to understand in music is that we have a series of 12 notes that repeat over and over called the *chromatic scale*.

Let's start by taking a look at an ascending chromatic scale starting on the note A. Here are the notes of an ascending chromatic scale in A: A–A#–B–C–C#–D–D#–E–F–F#–G–G#–A, etc.

Ascending Chromatic Scale in A

These are the notes of a descending chromatic scale in A: A–A♭–G–G♭–F–E–E♭–D–D♭–C–B–B♭–A, etc.

Descending Chromatic Scale in A

Following are a few important characteristics of the chromatic scale to remember:

* All notes in the chromatic scale are a half step apart

* Two half steps equal a whole step

* There are no sharps or flats between the notes B and C, or E and F

* One note can have two names. For instance: F# = G♭, D# = E♭, A# = B♭, etc. These are referred to as *enharmonic equivalents*.

* Any two notes, 12 notes apart, equal an octave, for instance, C to C, or E♭ to E♭, or G to G, etc.

Chromatic scales on the guitar are easy to visualize. You can play a chromatic scale on any string by striking the open string and playing notes on every fret up to the 12th fret. This applies, of course, to all six strings. All the notes, as you travel up the string one fret at a time are a half step apart. Every other fret on the guitar equals the distance of a whole step.

Chromatic Scale on One String

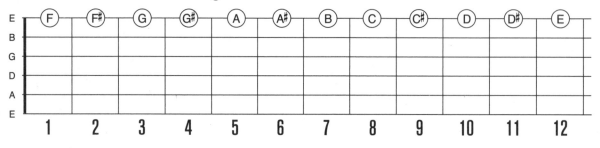

Here is an E Chromatic scale, covering three octaves on the fingerboard:

Major-Scale Fundamentals

Now that you are familiar with the chromatic scale and how basic intervals work, it's time to take a look at the *major scale*. The major scale is important because most Western music (classical, pop, rock, blues, jazz, etc.) is based on it.

Lots of guitarists want to play the "spicier" sounds associated with jazz and other improvised music, but it is essential to spend time studying the major scale to understand how it works first. To a large extent, your success with other scales and improvisational devices will depend on how solidly you understand the major scale. Most of the concepts and exercises involved with the major scale will also be used with other scales, so it pays to take your time with the major-scale fundamentals. As a result, it won't take as long to master other scales and devices later on.

The formula of steps for the major scale is: whole–whole–half–whole–whole–whole–half, or $1-1-\frac{1}{2}-1-1-1-\frac{1}{2}$.

We can plug this formula into the chromatic scale to create a major scale rooted on any note we choose. If we start the formula on C, we will create a C Major scale. Starting on F will produce an F Major scale, and so on. Below are two examples that illustrate this process.

Constructing a C Major Scale from the Chromatic Scale

(C–D–E–F–G–A–B–C)

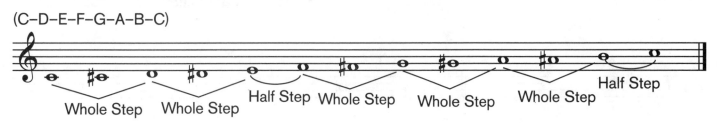

Constructing an F Major Scale from the Chromatic Scale

(F–G–A–B♭–C–D–E–F)

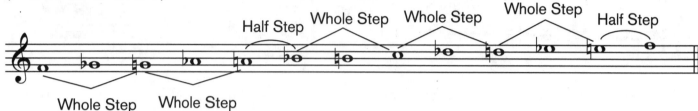

Since there are 12 notes in the chromatic scale, there are 12 possible major scales. As discussed on page 8, some notes have two names, like F♯ and G♭. Starting the major scale formula on either of these notes will produce the same scale in terms of sound, but they will be written differently. The F♯ version of the scale uses sharp signs, while the G♭ version uses flat signs instead.

Musicians normally think of there being 12 major scales, each one representing a different key. While you may occasionally run into a song written in the key of F♯ or C♯, for instance, you'll mostly be thinking in the following keys or scales:

Shown in the *cycle of 4ths**:

C–F–B♭–E♭–A♭–D♭–G♭–B–E–A–D–G

or shown in the *cycle of 5ths**:

G–D–A–E–B–G♭–D♭–A♭–E♭–B♭–F–C

Most players tend to think in and practice using the cycle of 4ths because so many chord progressions follow its pattern.

Here are all 12 major scales (in cycle of 4ths order) in musical notation and with letter names:

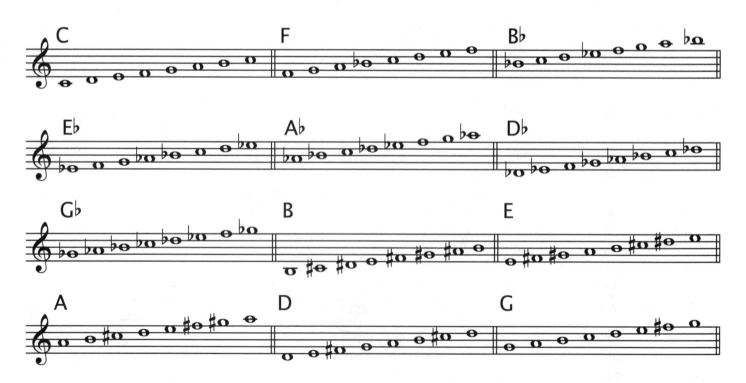

* Musicians often group keys or scales into perfect 4ths or 5ths. The two groupings here show the cycle of 4ths and cycle of 5ths.

C	D	E	F	G	A	B	C
F	G	A	B♭	C	D	E	F
B♭	C	D	E♭	F	G	A	B♭
E♭	F	G	A♭	B♭	C	D	E♭
A♭	B♭	C	D♭	E♭	F	G	A♭
D♭	E♭	F	G♭	A♭	B♭	C	D♭
G♭	A♭	B♭	C♭	D♭	E♭	F	G♭
B	C#	D#	E	F#	G#	A#	B
E	F#	G#	A	B	C#	D#	E
A	B	C#	D	E	F#	G#	A
D	E	F#	G	A	B	C#	D
G	A	B	C	D	E	F#	G

The Cycle of 4ths and 5ths

The chart below will make it easy for you to learn the cycle of 4ths. Read it counter clockwise for 4ths, clockwise for 5ths.

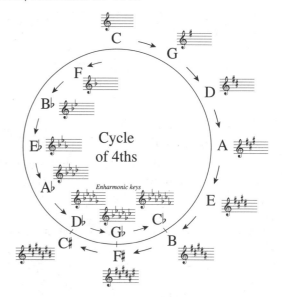

It is absolutely essential that you memorize the notes of all 12 major scales in the cycle of 4ths order. You must be able to recite these quickly. Your success in improvising, building chords, learning, memorizing, and transposing tunes depends on this. Did we say this was absolutely essential? What we really meant is it's **absolutely essential!** Really, it is.

You could simply memorize them by rote, or you may want to use this system:

The C Major scale has no sharps or flats—easy enough. The major scales for F through G♭ all use flat signs. The F Major scale has one flat, B♭. Each scale that follows F has one more flat than the previous scale, and the fourth note in each scale will be the newly flatted note. You just keep accumulating flats until you get to the G♭ Major scale, where all notes are flat except for F.

The major scales for B through G all use the sharp sign. The B Major scale has five sharps. Each scale that follows B will contain one less sharp than the previous scale, and the fourth note in each scale will be the newly dropped sharp.

Major-Scale Fingerings

There are quite a few systems for learning major-scale fingerings on the guitar, and most of them are thought out and logical. It is important to remember that these systems for learning are just that—systems for learning. Ultimately, when we play real music in real situations, these "systems" usually go by the wayside. By the time we have cultivated the ability to create spontaneous music, the systems we have practiced to help us learn the fingerboard actually become weights that hold us down. Still, systematic learning has an important place in our development. The ultimate goal is to see the fingerboard as a whole in terms of notes, arpeggios, scales, and chords. We need certain systems, or perspectives, to help us break down areas of the fingerboard for a while until we can see these things as a cohesive whole (this, however, takes much longer than we'd like).

If you are completely happy with your system of major-scale fingerings, there is no need to change anything as this will just prolong the overall learning process. On the other hand, if your major-scale chops are lacking in some way, or if you don't know at least five or six fingerings for the same scale, you have some work to do.

The system we'll cover here consists of six separate fingerings—two that begin with your 1st finger, two that begin with your 2nd finger, and two that begin with your 4th finger. When you have gained control of these fingerings, it will be possible to improvise in 11 different major keys without moving your hand out of position, no matter where you are positioned on the neck. Let's look at the labeling of each fingering.

This first fingering is called 1-E because the *root* (the note the scale is named after such as E in E Major) of the scale is found on the 6th, or low E, string and played with the 1st finger.

Major Scale Fingering 1-E (in C)

○ = Root

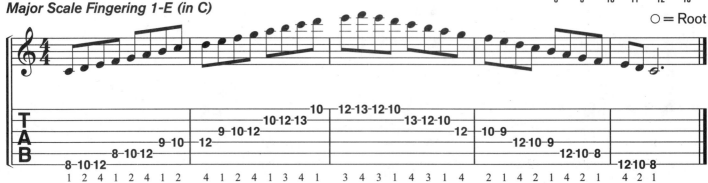

This fingering is called 2-E. Once again, the root is found on the 6th string, but this time it is played with the 2nd finger.

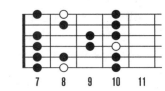

Major Scale Fingering 2-E (in C)

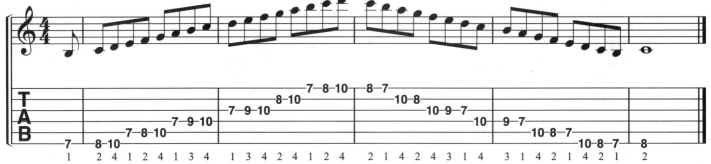

This is fingering 4-E. The root is played with the 4th finger on the 6th string. When you play the B note on the 4th string with your pinky, be sure to not move your whole hand. Just stretch with your finger and grab the note.

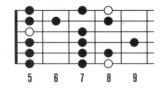

Major Scale Fingering 4-E (in C)

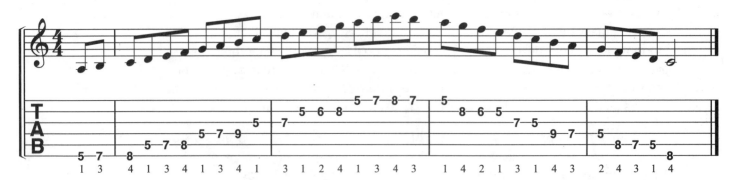

Here is fingering 1-A. Play the root of the scale with your 1st finger on the 5th, or A, string.

Major Scale Fingering 1-A (in C)

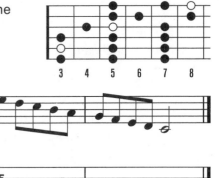

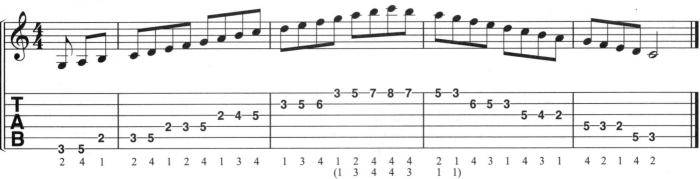

This is fingering 2-A. There are two common ways to finger the notes on the 1st string. Don't slide into the second note when you use the same finger for two consecutive notes. Sliding is an effect and should not be part of your normal way of fingering a scale (or arpeggio or lick, for that matter).

Major Scale Fingering 2-A (in C)

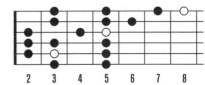

Here is fingering 4-A. This one is shown as an F Major scale so that the fingering lies more centrally on the fingerboard (in C Major, this fingering may not be reachable on all guitars). When you get to the shift on the 1st, or high E, string, your hand must move very smoothly so that these notes do not sound different in terms of volume or tone from the other notes in the scale. This takes some practice—listen very carefully.

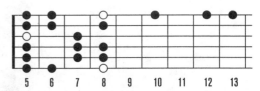

Major Scale Fingering 4-A (in F)

Musicians tend to use major scales for improvisation in many situations. This scale-fingering system we have been learning is quite useful when you have to improvise through many key centers rapidly.

Position

We define a *position* as the span of six frets. Generally, your 1st and 4th fingers cover two frets each, and your 2nd and 3rd fingers cover one (this idea is not carved in stone—there will be exceptions).

The following diagram illustrates the 11 major scales that are playable starting at the 3rd fret. Keep in mind that 11 different scale fingerings are possible no matter where your left hand is on the fingerboard.

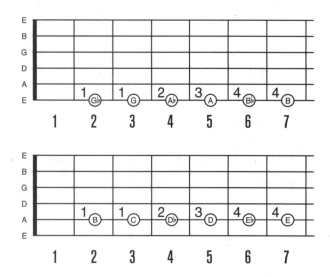

There will always be duplication of one key when you play in one six-fret area; in this case, the B scale is both at the 7th fret of the 6th string, and at the 2nd fret of the 5th string (as shown above). There will also be one key *not* in position—that key can be found one fret down on the 6th string or one fret up on the 5th string. After you have learned all the scale fingerings shown on pages 12 and 13, you should practice all the fingerings together in each position using the diagrams above as guides.

Joe Pass (1929–1994) was known for his extensive use of walking basslines, melodic counterpoint during improvisation, use of a chord-melody style of play and outstanding knowledge of chord progressions. He opened up new possibilities for jazz guitar and had a profound influence on future guitarists.

CHAPTER 2

You can construct any scale by plugging its formula into the chromatic scale as we did with the major scale. Chapters 2–5 will show you techniques that can be applied to any scale. Learning this thoroughly will give you a high level of control over the physical challenges of playing any scale and enable you to see the potential melodies that lurk beneath the surface. Once you have mastered these techniques using the major scale, you can apply them to any or all of the scales listed in Part 2 of this book.

How to Learn Scales

When learning new scale fingerings, the most important thing is to do so very slowly. It's easy to get excited about new sounds, but if you take it slowly, you will learn the scale better and avoid some common bad habits.

First, check your technique. You should play using your fingertips only, not the pads of your fingers, and make sure you place your fingertips directly behind the frets. Your fingers don't really play the notes—the frets do. Your finger's job is to press the string against the frets. This technique will save you physical exertion from pressing hard and also give you the truest and most accurate tone.

Try to keep your fingertips hovering just above the string. This is important. The higher you raise your fingers away from the fingerboard, the slower you play, simply because it takes longer for your finger to get to the string. You may not notice this so much when playing at slower tempos, but when you're trying to play fast, you'll find it makes a difference.

Be sure to practice your scales using alternate picking and that all the notes sound the same in terms of volume and tone. Again, this is important. If your picking is not dynamically even, you will get used to that sound. Eventually, you won't realize how uneven your sound is, but everyone else will!

When you start to learn a new fingering, many players prefer to learn and memorize the scale on just two strings at a time. First, practice the notes of the scale on only the 6th and 5th strings. Play them over and over, ascending and descending, until it feels comfortable. Start out slowly and gradually increase the speed. If you start to make mistakes, slow down—it's the only cure. Next, practice only the notes on the 4th and 5th strings the same way. When this feels easy, practice the scale pattern on the 6th, 5th, and 4th strings, listening again for evenness and accuracy. Then practice the notes on the 3rd and 4th strings, later adding the notes on the 6th and 5th strings. Continue this process through to the 1st string.

This should make learning and memorizing new fingerings much easier and less overwhelming. The example that follows shows this process with the 2-E C Major scale fingering. Vary the rhythms as you learn to keep things interesting.

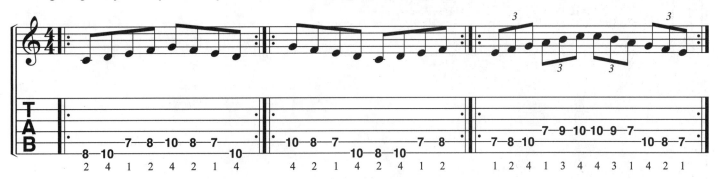

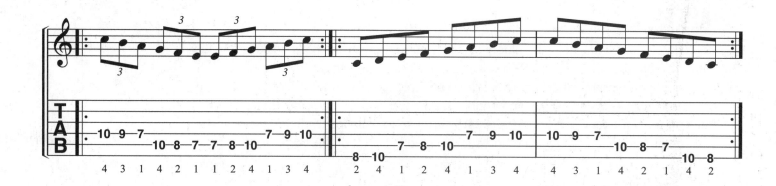

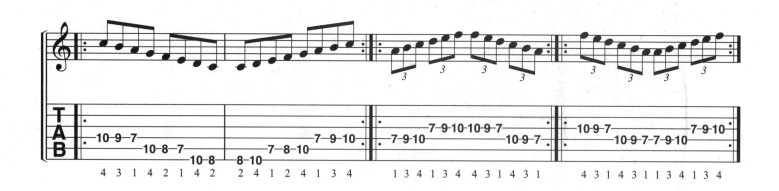

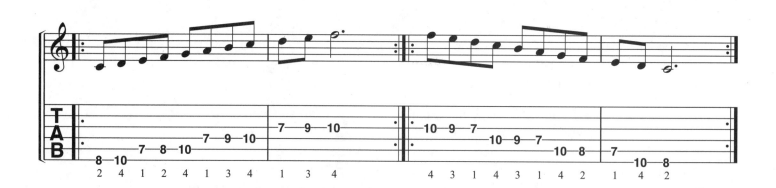

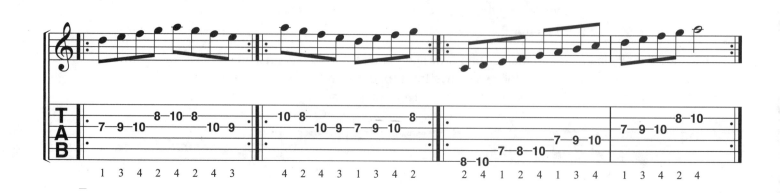

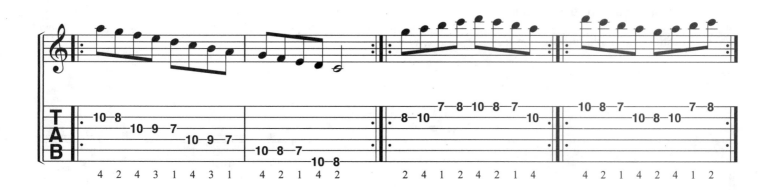

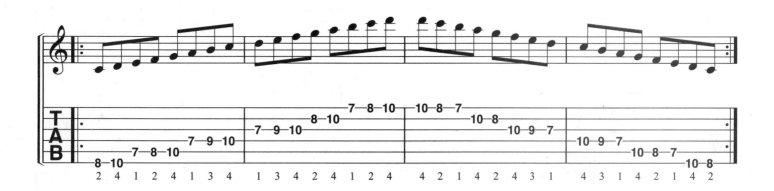

Practicing Scales

Practicing scales is an important part of learning any kind of music, but it can also be a trap. Some players practice scales endlessly for years, thinking that they are constantly improving. This isn't usually the case. Once you have really learned a scale (or lick or arpeggio), you need to end the mindless drilling and start making music with it instead. Of course, it will require time to learn and perfect a new scale fingering.

The process starting on page 18 is a great method for learning and getting comfortable with any scale fingering. Practice slowly and keep in mind that a single mistake means you are practicing too fast.

Kirk Hammett (born November 18, 1962) is the lead guitarist and a songwriter for Metallica and has been a member of the band since 1983. In 2003, Hammett was ranked 11th on Rolling Stone *magazine's list of The 100 Greatest Guitarists of All Time.*

PHOTO • KIRK HAMMETT AT METALLICA CONCERT

- Learn and memorize one scale fingering. When you can play the scale from memory 25 times in a row without flaws, you've learned it.

- Practice the scale fingering in the following ways:

Around the Cycle of 4ths

C Major

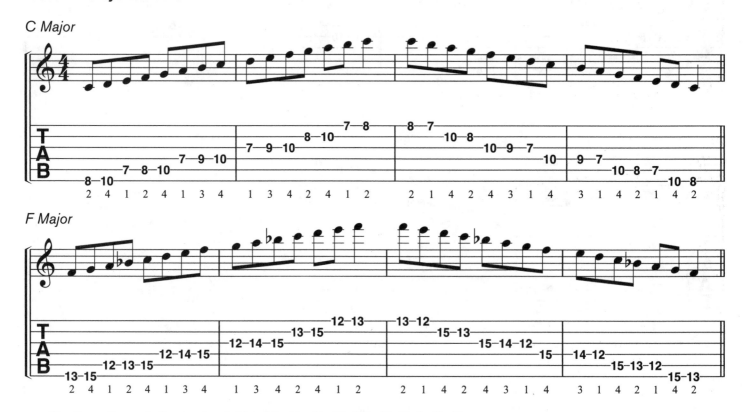

F Major

Continue through the cycle of 4ths: B♭–E♭–A♭–D♭–G♭–B–E–A–D–G.

Up and Down the Fingerboard Chromatically

G♭ Major

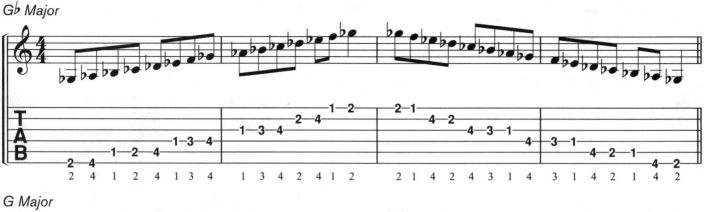

G Major

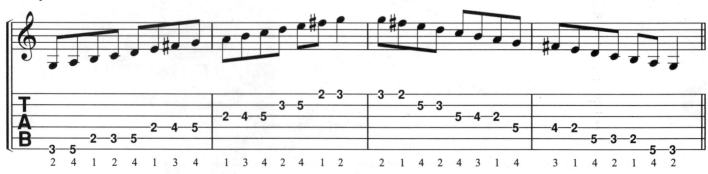

Continue moving up one fret at a time until you run out of frets, then descend the same way until you reach the 1st fret.

Up and Down the Fingerboard in Whole Steps

Gb Major

Ab Major

Continue moving up two frets at a time until you run out of frets, then descend the same way until you reach the 1st fret.

Up and Down the Fingerboard in Minor 3rds

Gb Major

A Major

Continue moving up three frets at a time until you run out of frets, then descend the same way until you reach the 1st fret.

Around the Cycle of 5ths

Continue through the cycle of 5ths: A–E–B–Gb–Db–Ab–Eb–Bb–F

Now, repeat all the previous steps starting on page 17, alternating between ascending and descending fingerings. In other words, if you were practicing the major scale around the cycle of 4ths, you would play an ascending C Major scale, followed by a descending F Major scale, followed by an ascending Bb Major scale, etc.

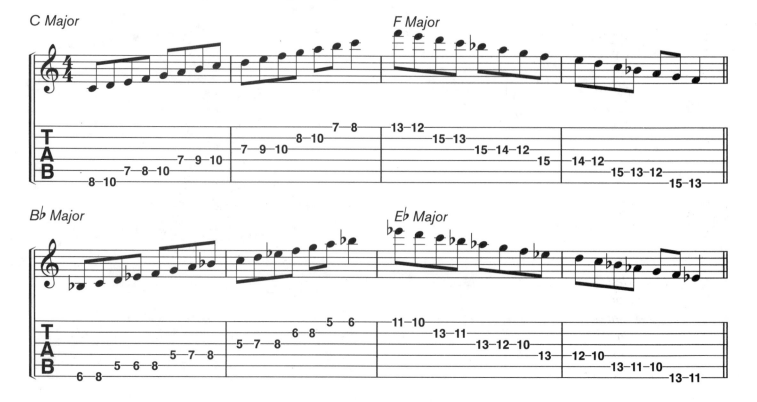

Or, using chromatic movement starting on G, you would play an ascending G scale followed by a descending A♭ scale, followed by an ascending A scale, and so on.

Continuing, do the following:

- Do the same thing with a second fingering.

- Learn more scales and follow the same routine.

- Do this for the rest of your life—this is a great way to burn licks and arpeggios into your fingers.

Realize that some things take a very long time to learn, as learning to play takes a lot of persistence. Expect that to be the case. Some things come easy—most things don't—but the feeling of having mastered something difficult makes it all worthwhile.

George Benson (b. 1943) is a Grammy Award-winning jazz guitarist, also known as a pop, R&B, and scat singer. He topped the Billboard 200 in 1976 with the triple-platinum album, Breezin'. *The most influential player in the generation after Wes Montgomery's, Benson uses a rest-stroke picking technique very similar to that of gypsy jazz players, such as Django Reinhardt.*

CHAPTER 3

How to Use Scales for Improvisation

Now that you know how to learn and practice scales, it's time to find ways to use scales for improvising.

In a typical scenario, an improvised guitar solo is based on the chord changes of the particular song you are playing. This means you have to know what scales work with what chords. It just so happens that most chords are derived from scales, so it's pretty easy to find out which chords work with a scale. We call this process *harmonizing a scale.* The chords that result from this process are referred to as the *diatonic harmonies.* Diatonic means "belonging to the key."

In the examples that follow, we will harmonize the major scale to find out what chords exist within it. When we harmonize a major scale, we stack 3rds on top of each scale degree. If we stack them three notes high, we get *triads.* If we stack them four notes high, we get *7th chords.*

Every major scale consists of seven chords—one rooted on each of the seven scale degrees. Here is a harmonized C Major scale:

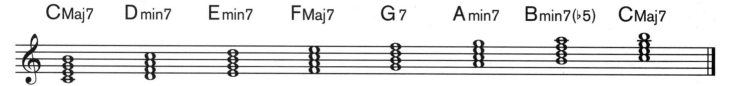

As you can see, this major scale produces two major 7th chords (on C and F), three minor 7th chords (on D, E, and A), one dominant 7th chord (on G), and one minor 7th flat-5 (half-diminished) chord (on B).

We also give each chord a Roman numeral designation. Chords that contain a major triad use upper-case Roman numerals, while chords that contain a minor 3rd use lower-case Roman numerals. The number 7 is commonly added to the V chord to designate that it is a dominant chord.

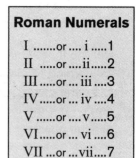

Roman Numerals
I ....or ..... i 1
II ......or ....ii 2
III ......or ... iii ...3
IV ......or ... iv 4
V ....or ..... v 5
VI ......or ... vi 6
VII ...or ...vii....7

This harmonic pattern is the same for all major scales. In other words, the I and IV chords in every major scale are major 7th chords. The ii, iii, and vi chords are always minor 7th chords. The V chord will always be dominant, and the vii chord will be a minor 7th flat-5 chord. The following example illustrates this pattern with the F and G Major scales:

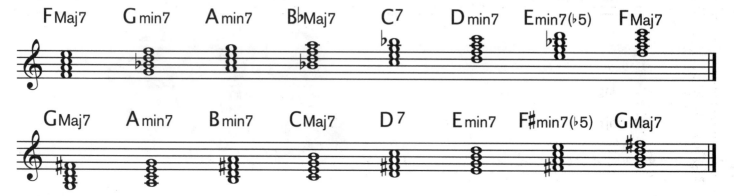

Practice reciting the chord names in every key, following the cycle of 4ths order. Simply say the notes in each scale with the chord names attached. For instance, for the key of B♭, recite: B♭Maj7–Cmin7–Dmin7–E♭Maj7–F7–Gmin7–Amin7♭5. This is one of the reasons you were asked to memorize the 12 major scales earlier. To a large extent, your success in future studies will depend on how well you know this material.

What you have just learned is that you can improvise with the major scale over any of the chords that are derived from it. In other words, a C Major scale can be used to improvise over CMaj7, Dmin7, Emin7, FMaj7, G7, Amin7, and Bmin7♭5. An F Major scale may be used to improvise over FMaj7, Gmin7, Amin7, B♭Maj7, C7, Dmin7, and Emin7♭5. And so on.

Practice improvising over the following chord progressions with the suggested major scales.

Improvise using a C Major scale.

Improvise using an F Major scale.

Improvise using a G Major scale.

Improvise with an F Major scale.

Improvise using a B♭ Major scale.

Improvise using a C Major scale.

Improvise using a C Major scale.

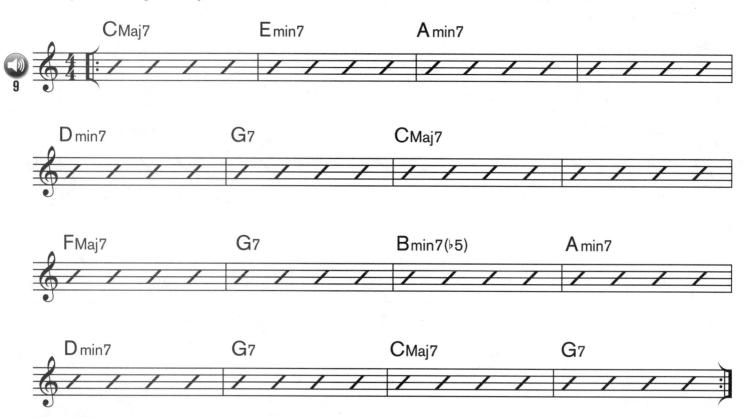

Eric Clapton at the Tsunami Relief concert in Cardiff's Millennium Stadium. Born in Surrey, England on March 30th, 1945, he has had tremendous success in the blues and rock world. His career spans work with such bands as Derek and the Dominos ("Layla") and Cream ("White Room"). He has also had solo hits, such as "Wonderful Tonight" and "Tears in Heaven."

CHAPTER 4

Targeting Chord Tones in Scales

If you have been working with the previous chord progressions and improvising using the correct major scale, you are probably starting to notice that your solos are sounding pretty good most of the time. But, you might also notice that it is possible to play a note from the scale that doesn't sound so great over a particular chord. This is because the best-sounding notes to use over a chord are the notes in the chord itself. This does not mean you should avoid using other notes in the scale.

Generally, you want to start your melodic line on a chord tone and use the non-chord notes to travel from chord tone to chord tone. This is known as *spelling out the chord changes.* While this can take a bit of time to perfect, the following method should help you accelerate the process.

Arpeggios are the notes in a chord played consecutively rather than simultaneously. In the approach shown here, you will learn all the arpeggios for the seven diatonic chords within a particular major-scale fingering.

Here is the major-scale fingering that the arpeggio fingerings will be based on (2-E in C):

C Major

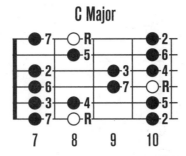

Here are the diatonic arpeggios and their corresponding chord shapes within this scale. Once you have learned the arpeggio shapes, practice them by playing the chord, followed by the arpeggio, and then the chord again. In time, you will learn to associate the arpeggio with the chord itself.

CMaj7 Arpeggio

I

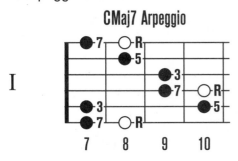

CMaj7

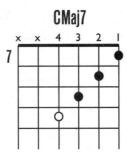

Dmin7 Arpeggio

ii

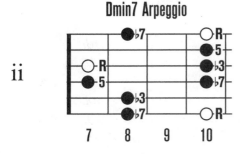

Dmin7

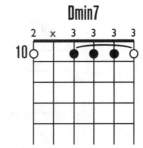

Emin7 Arpeggio

Emin7

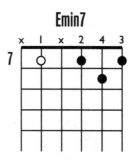

iii

Fmaj7 Arpeggio

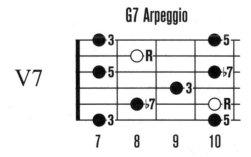

Fmaj7

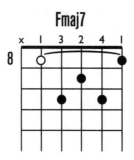

IV

G7 Arpeggio

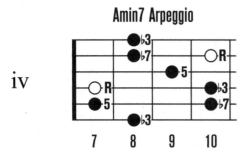

G7

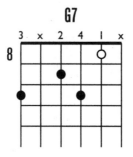

V7

Amin7 Arpeggio

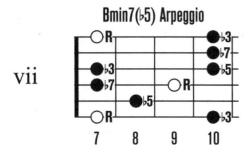

Amin7

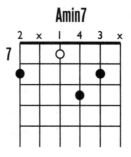

iv

Bmin7(♭5) Arpeggio

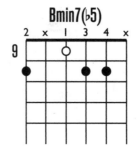

Bmin7(♭5)

vii

The first step to learning how to spell out changes is knowing your arpeggios. If you have memorized the previous set, it's time to move on. You could get started with the following material if you've memorized just a few of the arpeggios.

Many players begin improvising by randomly running up and down the scales that work over a particular chord progression. At some point, however, you need to start *playing through* instead of *playing over* the changes. Improvising with scales only gives the feeling of "playing over" or "floating over" the chord progression because you are playing random notes from the key center, which may or may not be found in the chord. Starting your lines on arpeggios will sound like you are playing "through" the progression because you are focusing on notes that are contained in both in the scale and the chord itself. It's simply a more interesting way to play. Your listeners will think so, too.

Here are five exercises that will get you started in this direction. You will need something to record on; software is ideal for the looping option. You could work on these exercises for many years. Take your time, but be sure to apply these same ideas to other scales and arpeggios you know.

Chord Tone Exercise 1

Learn to solo with chord tones only. Record one-chord vamps, so that you'll end up with seven different recordings—one for each diatonic chord. Then solo using only chord tones, but don't just stay in the key of C. Move these arpeggio shapes around to all roots. Yes, it sounds pretty bland at first, but the idea is to program your fingers and brain, so when you hear a Dmin7, for instance, all the D's, A's, F's, and C's, sort of light up all over the fingerboard for you. You will want to develop this view for all types of chords and arpeggios.

Next, record two-chord vamps and other simple diatonic progressions. Once again, try using only the chord tones of the chord being played at the time. Here are some sample progressions:

A ‖: CMaj7 | CMaj7 | Dmin7 | Dmin7 :‖   B ‖: CMaj7 | Dmin7 | Emin7 | Dmin7 :‖

C ‖: CMaj7 | Dmin7 | Emin7 | FMaj7 :‖   D ‖: Dmin7 | G7 | CMaj7 | Amin7 :‖

E ‖: Bmin7(♭5) | Emin7 | Amin7 | Amin7 :‖

F ‖: CMaj7 | Emin7 | Amin7 | Amin7 | Dmin7 | G7 | CMaj7 | CMaj7 |

    FMaj7 | G7 | Bmin7(♭5) | Amin7 | Dmin7 | G7 | CMaj7 | G7   :‖

Here is an example of how you might practice this chord-tone only approach with the sample progression A above.

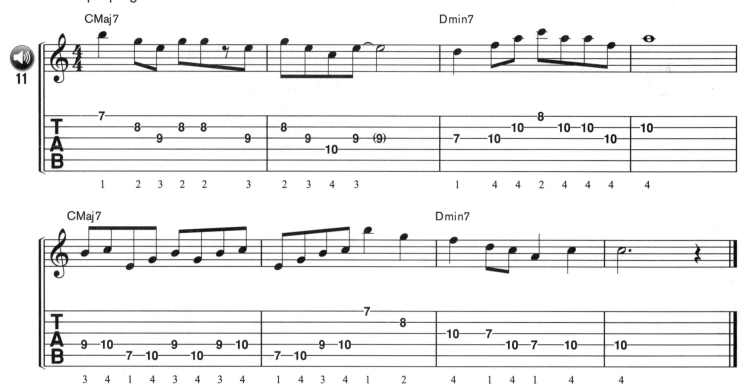

Chord Tone Exercise 2

When Exercise 1 starts to become easy for you (at least in one position), it's time to put the entire scale back to work again. Now, what you're going to do is improvise over the previous progressions using the entire major scale, but with each chord change you will begin your line on a chord tone. Start with roots, then 3rds, then 5ths, and finally 7ths.

For example, in measure 1 of progression F above, begin your melodic line on one of the CMaj7 chord tones (C–E–G–B), then move on to use the other notes in the scale. When you get to measure 2, your line will begin with an Emin7 chord tone (E–G–B–D). When you get to measure 3, your line will begin with a note found in an Amin7 chord (A–C–E–G), and so on. More simply put: Try to start on a chord tone every time the chord changes in the progression.

In most jazz applications, beginning your melody lines on the 3rds and 7ths of the chord will spell out the changes very effectively. This is because of the defining nature of 3rds and 7ths in all chords (these tones define the quality of the chord—whether they are major, minor, or dominant). In styles other than jazz, it is common to begin on any chord tone. In the next example, these tones are labeled.

This concept may seem a little rigid at first, but after some experience with this technique, you'll know when and where it will have the most tasteful effect.

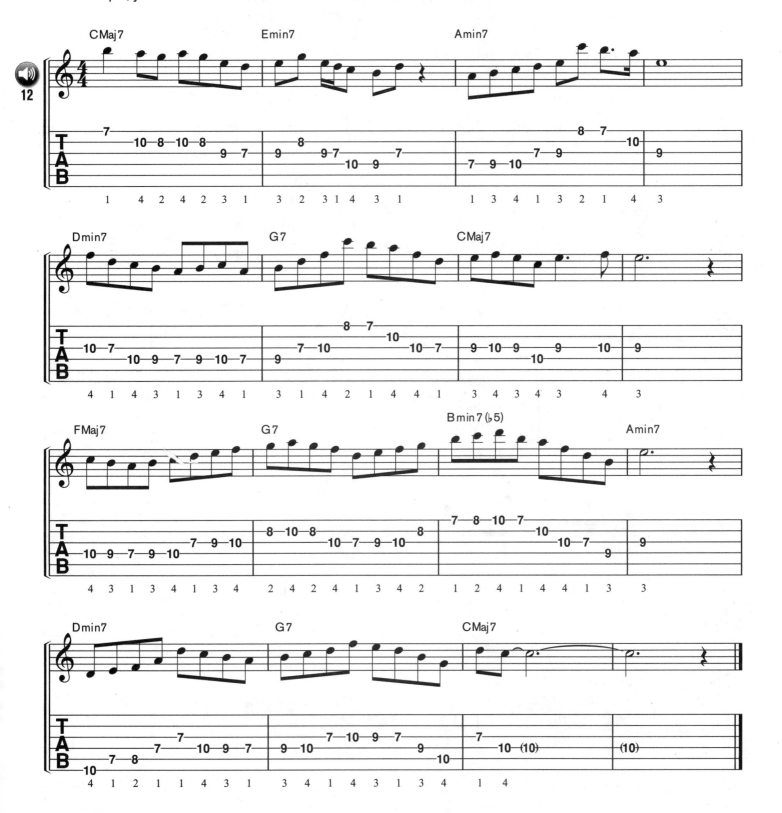

* The 9th is not a chord tone in this case. What do you think of the way it sounds? Nice, isn't it? More on this later.

Chord Tone Exercise 3

Use the same progressions again, but this time you'll approach the starting chord tone with its *lower neighbor*. For now, we'll define a lower neighbor tone as a note that is a half step below any chord tone.

For now, you want the chord tone to land on beat 1 of the measure, which means the lower neighbor tone must be played on the "&" of beat 4 from the previous measure. You'll do this each time the chord changes in the progression. Be sure to record at slow tempos, because this concept may not be easy at first. The lower neighbors are circled.

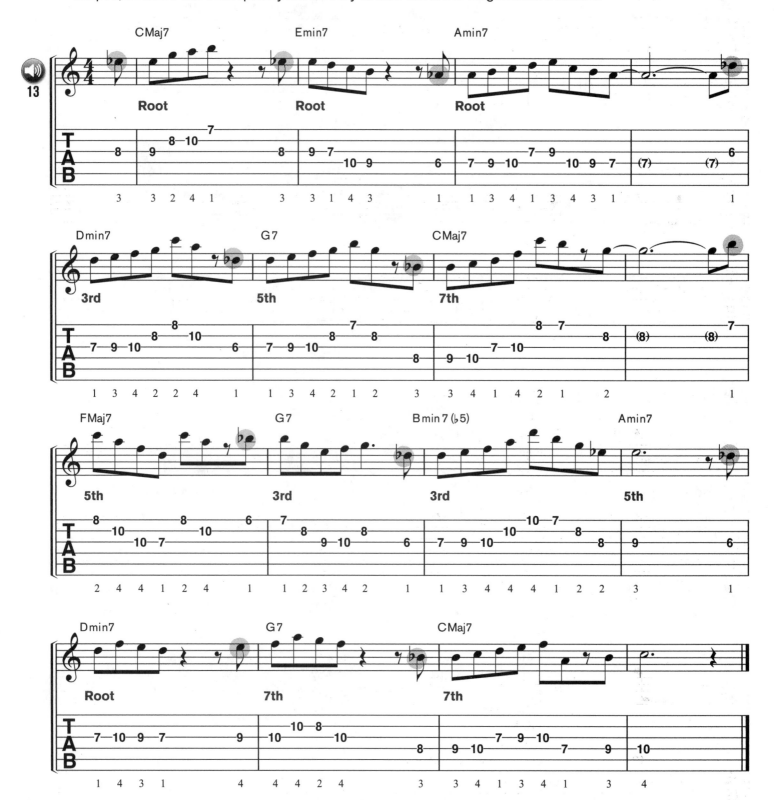

Chord Tone Exercise 4

This is the same as Exercise 3 but with *upper neighbor tones* instead. For now, we'll define an upper neighbor tone as a note that is one scale tone above any chord tone. The neighbor tones are circled.

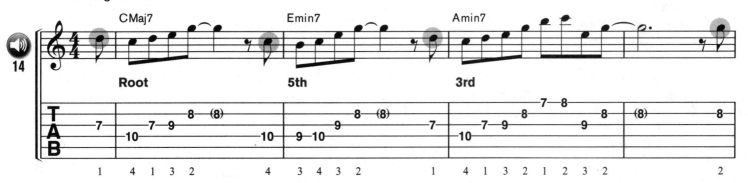

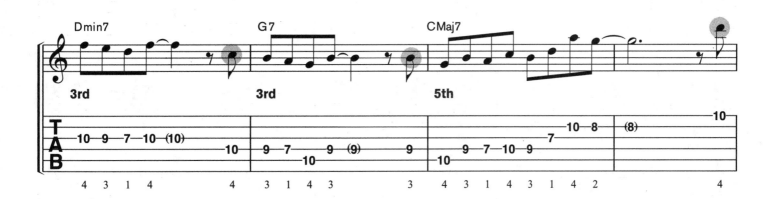

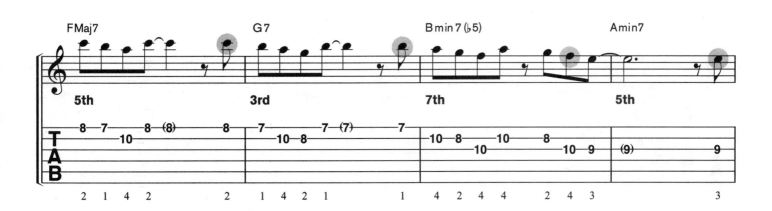

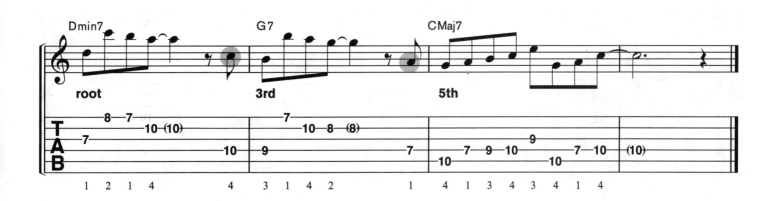

Chord Tone Exercise 5

With the same chord progressions you've been using for the previous exercises, you're going to apply both upper and lower neighbor tones in Exercise 5. Once again, you want the chord tone to land on beat 1 of the measure. This means one of the neighbor tones must be played on beat 4 while the other neighbor tone must be on the & of beat 4 of the previous measure. You'll do this every time the chord changes in the progression. Again, be sure to record at slow tempos to start. Both neighbor tones are circled.

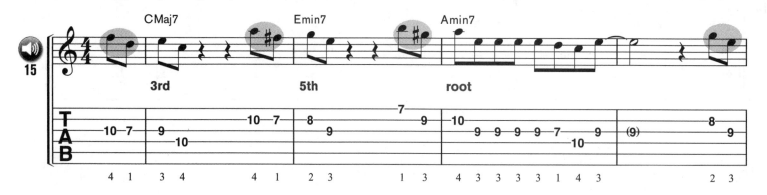

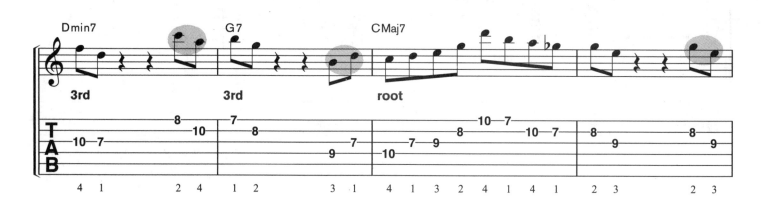

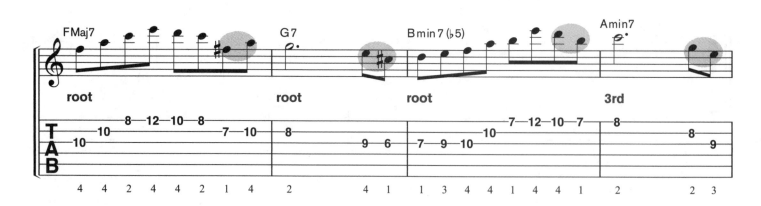

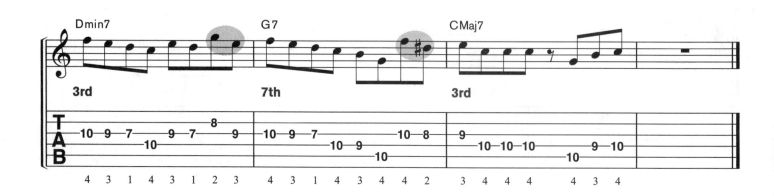

Effective Use of Chord Tones

At some point, you'll start to become familiar with recognizing chord tones all over the fingerboard.

Here are your new options for improvising:

- Start scalar lines on chord tones as the chords change in a progression

- Approach chord tones with a lower neighbor tone

- Approach chord tones with an upper neighbor tone

- Approach chord tones with both upper and lower neighbor tones

This is a long-term project. Take small bites at first to fully digest everything, and gradually apply these concepts to the music you play.

PHOTO COURTESY OF RUTGERS UNIVERSITY, INSTITUTE OF JAZZ STUDIES

Wes Montgomery (1923–1968) was one of the most important jazz guitarists, emerging after such seminal figures as Django Reinhardt and Charlie Christian. He influenced countless others, including Pat Martino, George Benson, Emily Remler, Kenny Burrell, and Pat Metheny.

CHAPTER 5

As mentioned earlier, beside scales, there are many musical tools and devices we can use to play improvised music. Licks, patterns, and spontaneous ideas all come into play. Most people start out by using scales, and there are many ways to find the good melodies hidden within them. Hopefully, the ideas introduced in this chapter will change the way you look at the scales you use for improvisation.

Developing Melodic Ideas from Scales

Diatonic Sequencing

Diatonic sequencing is taking a melodic line that works for a single chord and using it for all the diatonic chords in the key. Begin by playing a line that sounds good over the I chord, and then raise each note up one scale tone. You now have created a line that will work over the ii chord. Repeat this process from the second chord, and you will have a line for the iii chord. Continue this process for each chord in the scale.

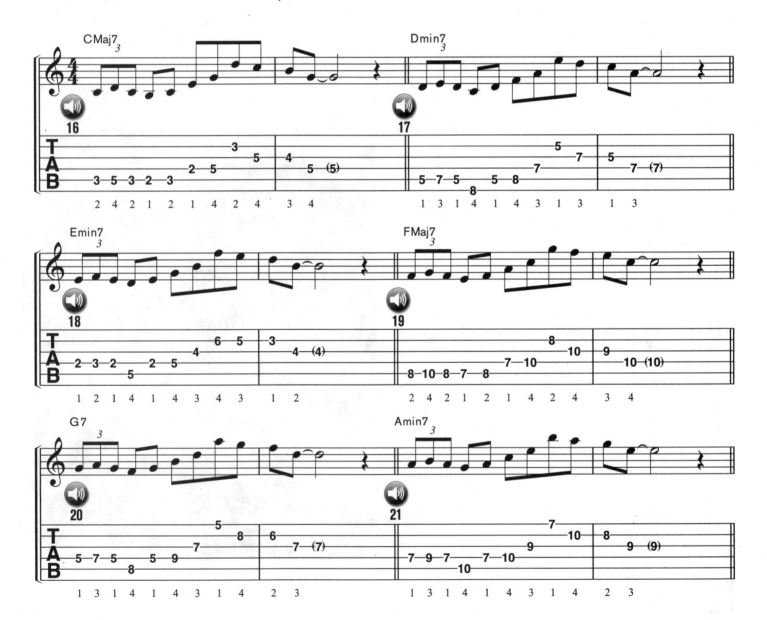

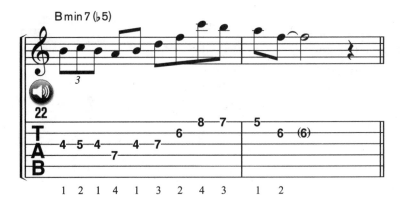

Sequences or Melodic Patterns

Using sequences or melodic patterns is a mathematical way to extract melodies from scales. Practicing these will help you develop both hands, and you'll start to hear more melodic possibilities.

Sequences will give your solos a sense of continuity and can also provide "filler" between the more dramatic sections of your solos. You can use them as inspiration for your own spontaneous ideas, and they can help you create longer melody lines—which is a sign of more advanced soloing.

You will want to learn a lot of these. Simply choose a pattern of notes beginning with the root of the scale, then raise each note by one scale tone. Generally, the smaller the melodic range you pick for your pattern, the more traditional it will sound. Wider intervallic leaps in your pattern will give you a more contemporary sound.

Try to learn one new pattern each week. This will get you into the habit of always looking for more melodic ideas. Sometimes these can take a while to learn, so have patience and try to insert them in your solos right away. Here are six common sequences you might want to learn:

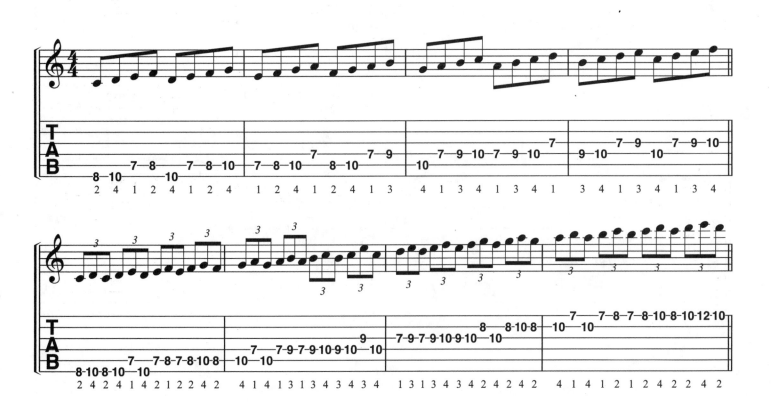

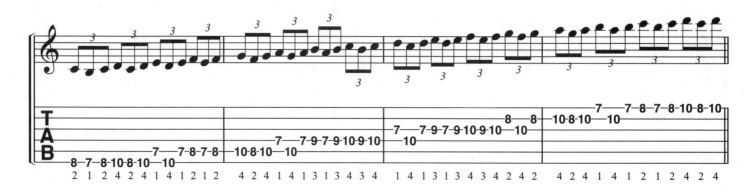

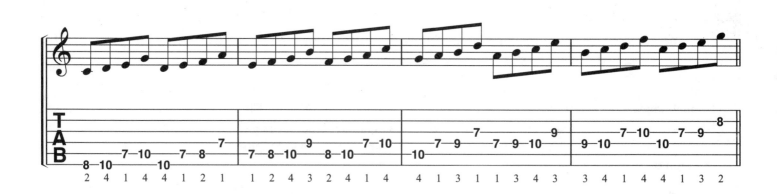

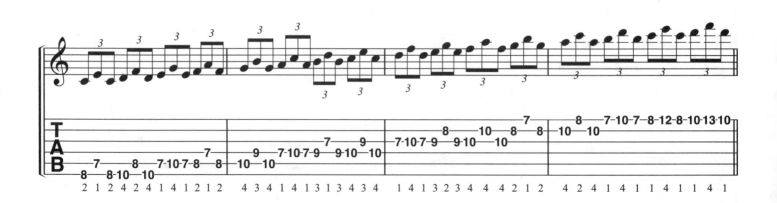

Chromaticism

So far, we have looked at ways to work with scales, chord tones, melodic patterns, and adding upper and lower chord tones. Another popular technique for expanding the possibilities of any scale is the use of *chromaticism,* or playing notes of the chromatic scale. This concept should be done with care and taste, as it is easy to go a little overboard. The key here is to begin your line with a chord tone found in the scale and lead into another chord tone with the chromatic notes found in between. Since this example is in the key of C, all flat and sharp notes are the chromatic notes.

Looking for Ideas on Adjacent Strings

A fun way to look for melodic ideas in your scales is to explore note combinations on adjacent strings. Let's look at C Major scale fingering 1-E, beginning on the highest two strings. Starting on the B string, we could play the notes G, A, B, C, and D on these two adjacent strings. Now, try to find four-note combinations that sound good to you. Following are a few ideas to get you started.

On the 1st and 2nd Strings (E and B)

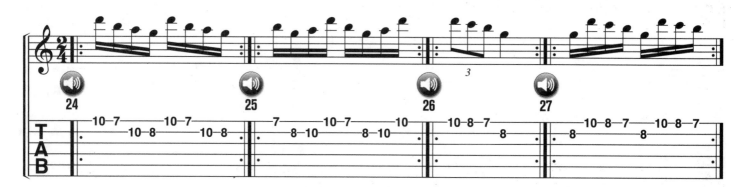

On the 2nd and 3rd Strings (B and G)

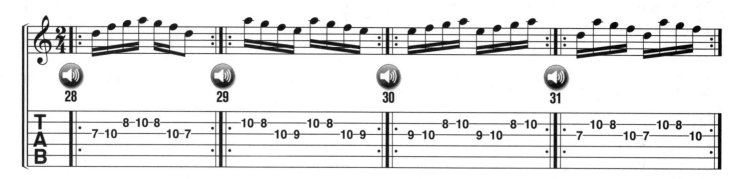

On the 3rd and 4th Strings (G and D)

On the 4th and 5th Strings (D and A)

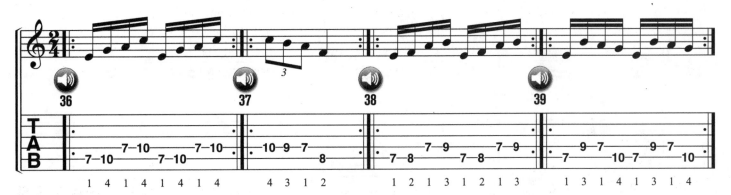

On the 5th and 6th Strings (A and E)

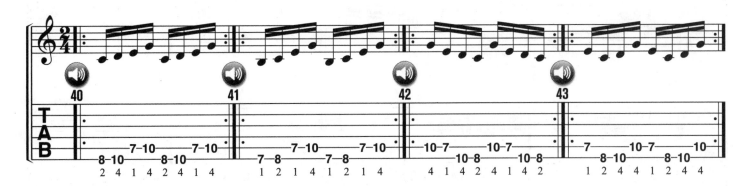

String Skipping

This is the same concept as the previous, except it involves every other string as opposed to two adjacent strings. Below are some ideas to get you started.

On the 1st and 3rd Strings (E and G)

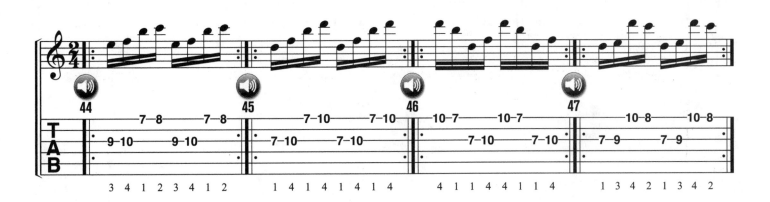

On the 2nd and 4th Strings (B and D)

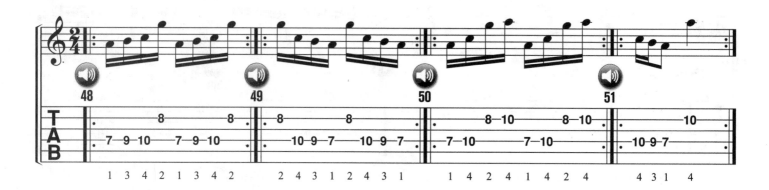

On the 3rd and 5th Strings (G and A)

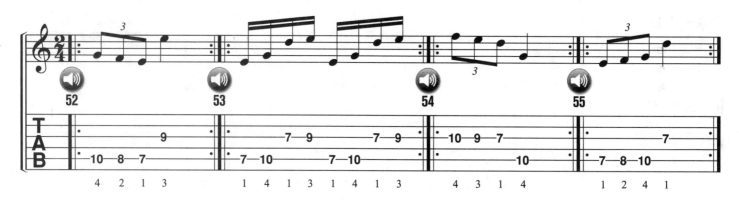

On the 4th and 6th Strings (D and E)

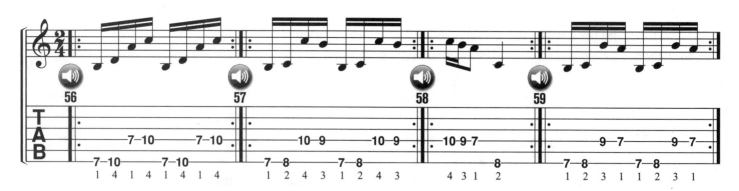

CHAPTER 6

Now What?

So far, you have put the major scale through a lot of changes. We've covered how to construct the scale, how to learn it, how to practice it, and how to get the most out of it for the purpose of improvising solos. You can now apply these concepts to every scale discussed in the second half of this book and those you learn going forward. This will allow you to have as much control over your melodic lines as possible.

Since we started out with the major scale, it would make sense to now start working on the minor scales and modes. There are three minor scales that correspond to every major tonality. They are the *natural minor scale*, *harmonic minor scale*, and *melodic minor scale*. We'll begin with the natural minor scale.

> **Modes**
> A *mode* is simply a reordering of a scale. A mode of the major scale has all the same notes as the major scale, but they are played in a different order. Thus, each mode has its own, unique sound.

The Natural Minor Scale

The *natural minor scale* is the same as the Aeolian mode, which is built on the 6th degree of the major scale. To create a natural minor scale, start with the 6th degree of the major scale and play all the notes of that major scale until you reach the octave note of the 6th degree. Essentially, the 6th degree of the major scale becomes the 1st degree of the natural minor scale, which results in a new formula of steps: whole–half–whole–whole–half–whole–whole. Consequently, scale degrees 3, 6, and 7 are one half step lower than they would be in a major scale, making them ♭3, ♭6, and ♭7.

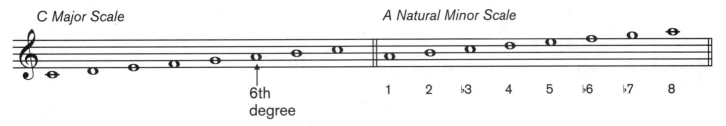

Here are two useful fingerings for the natural minor scale. Be sure to practice them in all 12 keys.

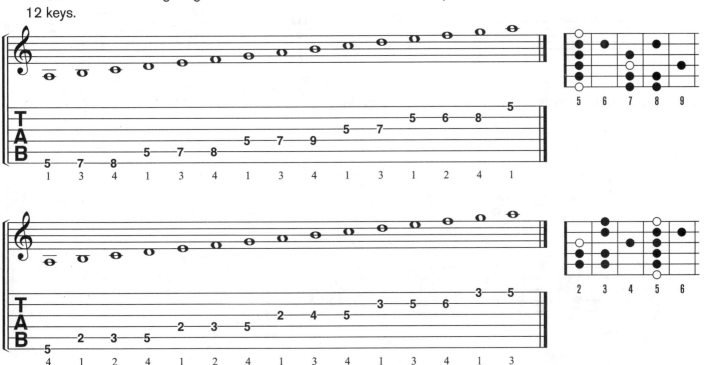

Like the major scale, each minor scale produces a series of diatonic chords. Since there are three different minor scales, there are three different sets of diatonic minor chords. Music written in minor keys often combines the chords from all three minor scales, so it's a good idea to be familiar with each set.

The Harmonized Natural Minor Scale

Obviously, the chords produced by the natural minor scale are identical to those of the relative major scale because both scales contain the same notes. However, their Roman numerals change: the vi of the major scale becomes the i of the minor scale, vii becomes ii, and so on.

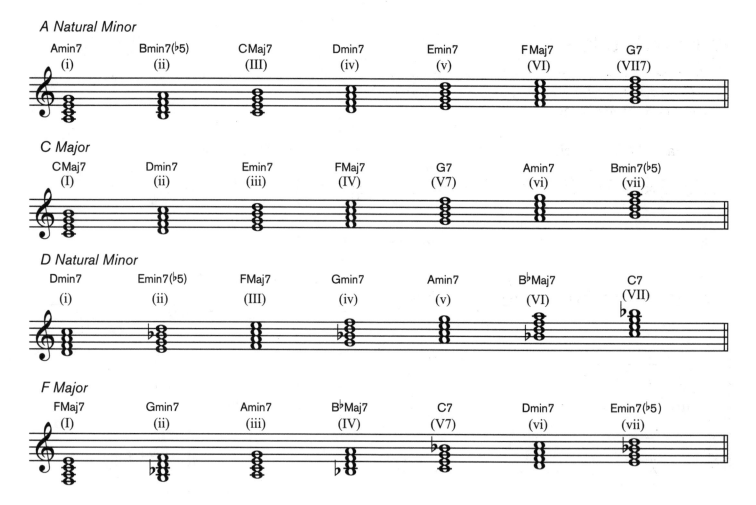

Here are two harmonized natural minor scales to play. Practice them in all keys.

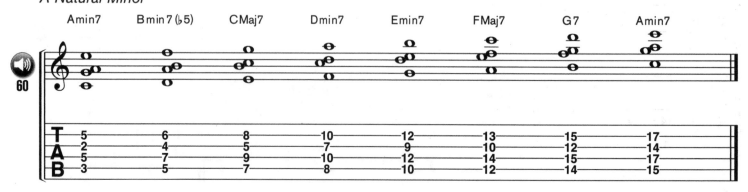

D Natural Minor

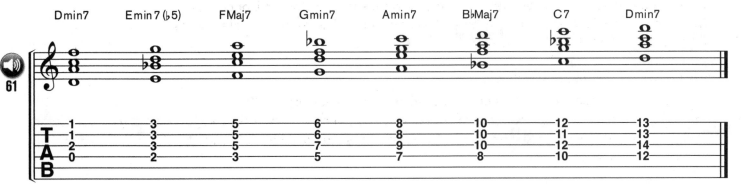

The Harmonic Minor Scale

When we want to create a *harmonic minor scale*, we simply start with a natural minor scale and then raise the 7th degree (which gives us a ♮7). Altering this note gives us a much more "exotic" minor scale.

A Natural Minor Scale   *A Harmonic Minor Scale*

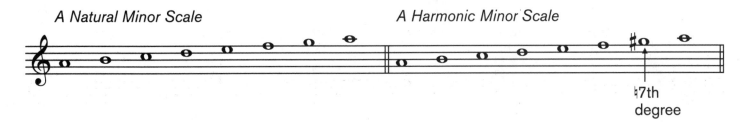

♮7th degree

Here are two fingerings for the A Harmonic Minor scale:

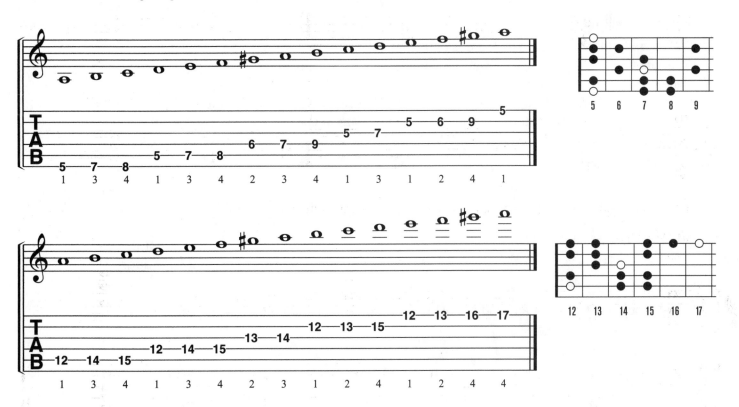

The Harmonized Harmonic Minor Scale

Here are two fingerings for harmonized harmonic minor scales. The raised 7th degree in this scale creates a different set of chords from natural minor.

A Harmonic Minor Scale

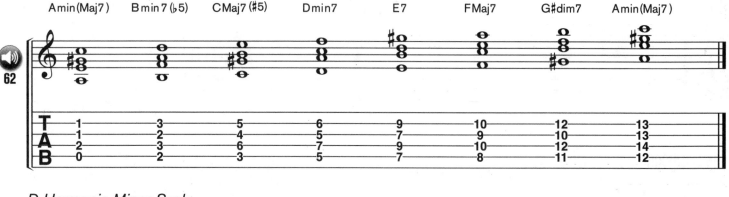

D Harmonic Minor Scale

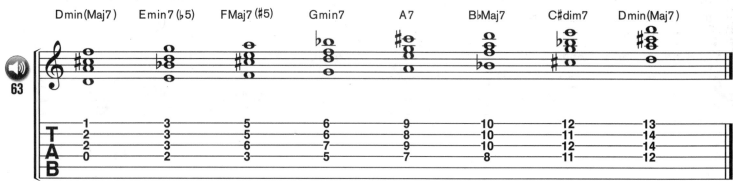

The Melodic Minor Scale

We'll raise both the 6th and 7th degrees of the natural minor scale (giving us a ♮6 and ♮7) to produce a *melodic minor scale*. The traditional melodic minor scale descends differently than it ascends. It descends as a natural minor scale. The scale shown here includes only the ascending portion and it is played the same descending. For that reason, in non-classical contexts, it is sometimes called *jazz minor*.

A Harmonic Minor Scale   *A Melodic Minor Scale*

Note: You can also create a melodic minor scale by lowering the 3rd of any major scale.

Here are two fingerings for melodic minor scales. Again, practice this in all keys.

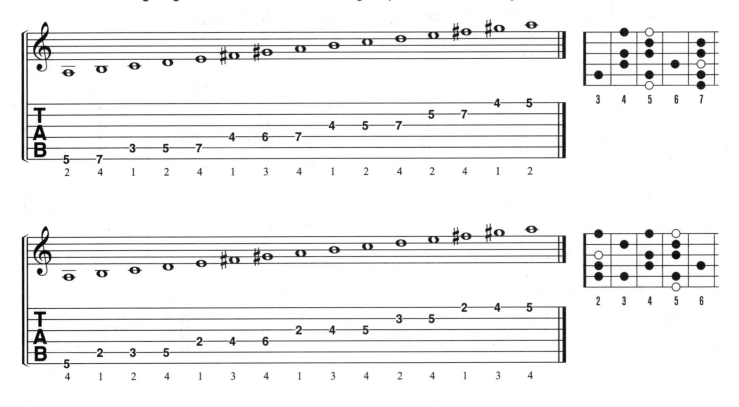

The Harmonized Melodic Minor Scale

A Melodic Minor Scale

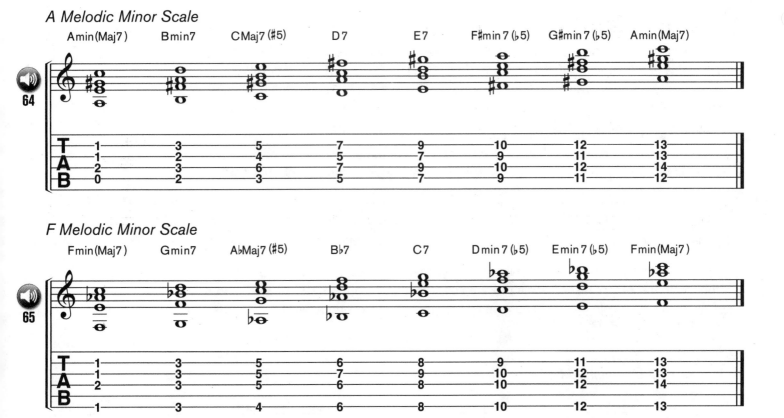

F Melodic Minor Scale

Working with the Melodic Minor Scale

The melodic minor scale has several interesting applications. First, like the major scale, it may be used over any of the chords generated from it but with one important difference: Any line you play from the melodic minor scale will work equally well over *any* of the chords constructed from it. There are no "avoid notes" with this scale. Melody lines played using this scale might result in a dramatic sound, depending on which chord you are playing over, but it'll always work and sound good.

If you play this scale one half step above the root of a dominant chord (Ab Melodic Minor over an altered G7 chord, for instance), the scale will contain all the possible alterations of that chord (G7b5, G7#5, G7b9, G7#9, G7b5b9, G7#5#9, G7b5#9, and G7#5b9). For this reason, many jazz musicians use this scale almost exclusively for playing over these types of chords.

Other Important Scales for Altered Chords

The Whole-Half Diminished Scale

The *diminished scale* is a *symmetrical scale* (a scale whose notes divide the octave into equal parts) whose step formula is: whole–half–whole–half–whole–half–whole–half, etc.

G Whole-Half Diminished Scale

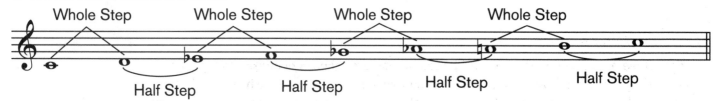

The diminished scale is useful in two different applications. As you would guess from the name, it can be used to improvise over diminished chords. In this case, you use the diminished scale that shares the root of the diminished chord over which you are improvising.

You can also use the diminished scale to improvise over altered dominant chords. In this case, we start the scale one half step above the root of the altered chord being played. In other words, we would use an Ab Diminished scale over an altered G7 chord, a Db Diminished scale over an altered C7 chord, and so on.

To find out exactly which altered chords the diminished scale works well with, write the scale out and analyze how each scale degree relates to the chord.

In the example below, we see an Ab Diminished scale used over an altered G7 chord. In this case, the Ab Diminished scale provides us with a b9, #9, and b5(#11) of a G7 chord. This means the scale can be used to improvise over the following altered G7 chords: G7b9, G7#9, G7b5, G7#11, G7b5b9, and G7b5#9.

Ab Whole-Half Diminished Scale Over G7 (alt)

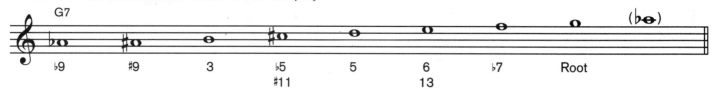

One of the cool things about diminished scale fingerings is that you can move them around the fingerboard in minor 3rd intervals, and they will always contain the same notes. So, you can use the diminished scale all over the fingerboard quite easily. Check out the fingerings that follow:

A♭ Whole-Half Diminished Scale

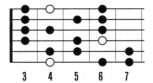

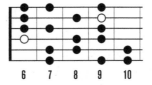

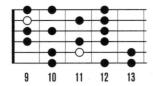

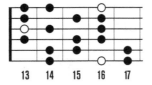

The Whole Tone Scale

The *whole tone scale* is another useful scale to use over altered dominant chords. It's another symmetrical scale with a step formula that supports its name: whole–whole–whole–whole–whole–whole–whole–whole, etc. To use it over an altered dominant chord, simply start the whole tone scale from any chord tone.

Here is how the whole tone scale stacks up over an altered G7 chord:

G Whole Tone Scale over G7(alt)

We now see that the whole tone scale can be used over a G7♭5, G7♯11, G9♭5, G9♯5, or G7♭5♭13 chord.

Below are three fingerings for the whole tone scale:

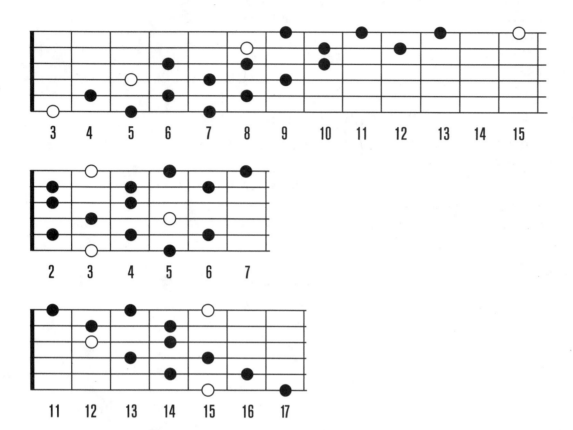

Very Important Information

As you look through Part 2 of this book, it can be easy to become overwhelmed by all the different scales, not to mention their usage. Try to remember this: there probably isn't a player alive that would use *all* of these scales. There are certain scales that all players use to some extent and some scales that are used only rarely.

With this in mind, the following list would be considered the most useful scales to the most players. You should have several different fingerings for all these scales under your fingers and be comfortable playing them in every key. Consider finding a number of different scale dictionaries or encyclopedias, such as *The Ultimate Guitar Chord and Scale Encyclopedia* (40140), to learn the fingerings for them.

The Most Useful and Versatile Scales

- Major Scale
- Modes of the Major Scale: especially Dorian and Mixolydian
- Natural Minor Scale
- Harmonic Minor Scale
- Melodic Minor Scale
- Modes of the Melodic Minor Scale (Dorian ♭2, Lydian Augmented, Lydian ♭7, Mixolydian ♭6, Locian ♯2, Super Locrian)

- Major and Minor Pentatonic Scales
- Blues Scales
- Diminished Scales
- Whole Tone Scales
- Lydian-Dominant Scales

CONTENT DETAILS FOR PART 2

1. **In the left column, look up the chord type** you would like to solo over and learn which scales it works with. On those pages, you'll also find two to four voicings for the chord, and two fingerings for the scale.

2. **In the right column, look up the scale** you're interested in learning and discover which chord types it works with in a solo. Again, on those pages, you'll also find two fingerings for the scale, and two to four voicings for the chord.

Understanding the Chord and Scale Charts

Function means the scale degree this chord is used with, such as I or vi.

This chord will appear in either a major or minor key, or both.

Indicates the tone on which the scale is built. We don't always use a scale built on the root of the chord. For instance, we might start on the 9th, or the 4th.

Chord and Scale Chart

Chords	Function	Major or Minor Key	Scale or Mode	Starting on…

A scale that can be used with this chord.

PART 2: SCALES OVER CHORDS

In Part 1, you learned how to learn and practice scales using major-scale fingerings. All of those concepts can apply to any scale. Part 2 is a resource that will help you quickly look up any chord and learn what scales will work over it. Many different scales are included here, and you will have many opportunities to apply everything you learned in Part 1.

In Part 2, two to four voicings are given for each chord and there are many other possibilities. Two fingerings are shown for each scale, too, but again, many more possibilities exist. The information in Part 2 will get you started with lots of chord voicings and the scales to use for improvising over them. Do your best to apply the methods you learned in Part 1, and you'll have an excellent start as an improvising guitarist.

Each section includes a chart to help you understand the chord types. It shows how they function in a major or minor key, the types of scales that work over them, and on which chord tone to base the scale. See the bottom of page 49 to better understand the charts.

MAJOR CHORDS
Unaltered*   Major, 6, Maj7, Maj9, and Maj13 Chords

You can also use the major pentatonic scale from the 9th of a IV chord in major keys.

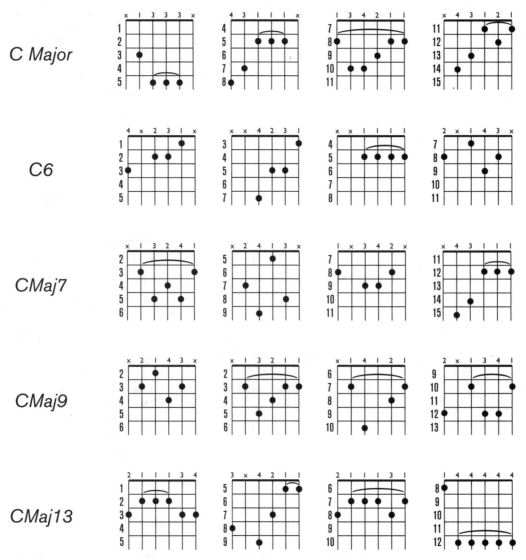

* Some major-type chords have altered tones (♯5, ♭5, ♯9, ♭9). For information on altered major chords, see page 53.

Chord and Scale Chart

Chords		Function	Major or Minor Key	Scale or Mode	Starting on...
All unaltered major chords	{	I	Major	Major	The root of the chord
Major, 6, Maj7	{	I or IV	Major	Major Pentatonic	The root of the chord
Maj9, Maj13	{	I or IV	Major	Major Pentatonic	The 5th of the chord
	{	IV	Major	Major Pentatonic	The 9th of the chord
	{	IV	Major	Lydian	The root of the chord
Maj7		VI	Minor	Lydian#2	The root of the chord

Major

Use a major scale from the root of a I chord in major keys.

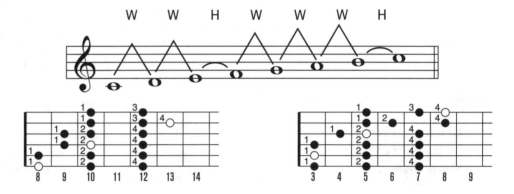

Major Pentatonic

Use a major pentatonic scale from the root of a I chord or the root of IV chord in major keys.

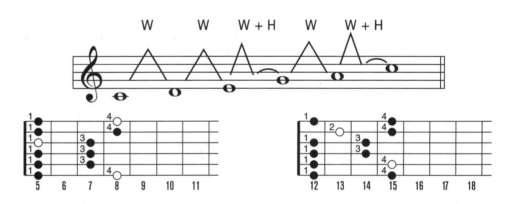

You can also use the major pentatonic scale starting on the 5th of a I or a IV chord in major keys.

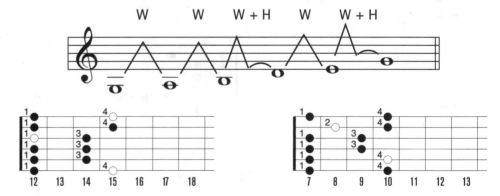

You can also use the major pentatonic scale from the 9th of a IV chord in major keys.

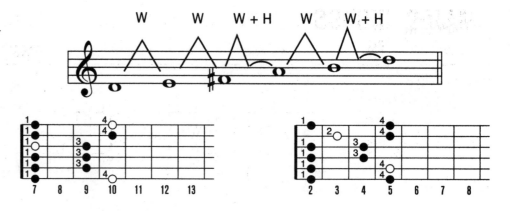

Lydian

Use the Lydian mode starting on the root of the IV chord in major keys.

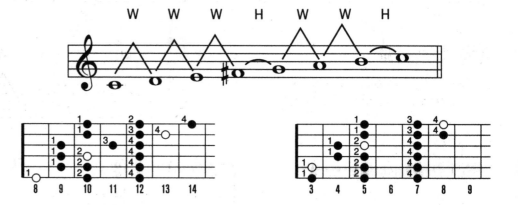

Lydian #2

Use a Lydian #2 mode starting on the root of a Maj7 when it functions as a VI chord in a minor key.

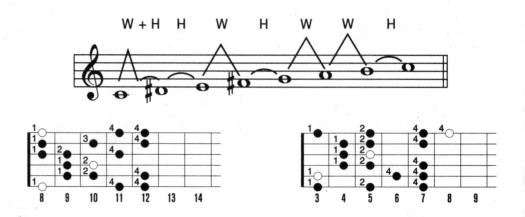

MAJOR CHORDS
Altered

Maj7#5 Chords

C Maj7#5

Chord and Scale Chart

Chords	Function	Major or Minor Key	Scale or Mode	Starting on…
Major7#5 {	Any	Both	Lydian Augmented	The root of the chord
	Any	Both	Ionian #5	The root of the chord

Lydian Augmented

Use a Lydian Augmented mode starting on the root of a Maj7#5 chord.

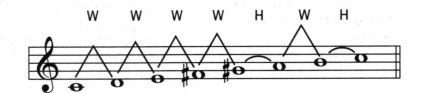

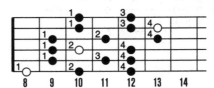 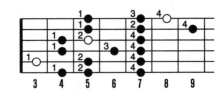

Ionian #5

Use the Ionian #5 mode starting on the root of a Maj7#5 chord.

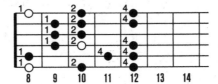 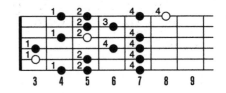

Maj7♭5, Maj7#11, and Maj9#11 Chords

CMaj7♭5

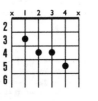

CMaj7#11

CMaj9#11

Chord and Scale Chart				
Chords	Function	Major or Minor Key	Scale or Mode	Starting on...
Maj7♭5, Maj7♯11, { Any	Any	Both	Major Pentatonic	The 9th of the chord
Maj9♯11	Any	Both	Lydian	The root of the chord

Major Pentatonic (from the 9th)

Use a major pentatonic scale starting on the 9th of a Maj7♭5, Maj7♯11, or Maj9♯11 chord.

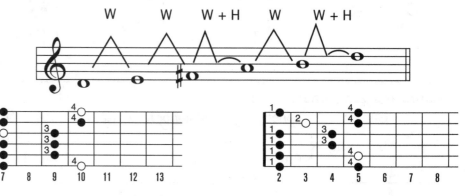

Lydian

Use the Lydian mode starting on the root of a Maj7♭5, Maj7♯11, or Maj9♯11 chord.

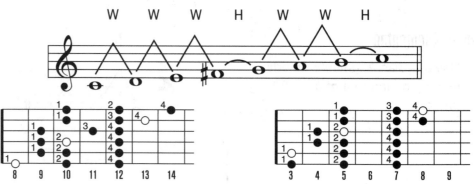

Maj7♯5♯11 Chords

C Maj7♯5♯11

Chord and Scale Chart				
Chords	Function	Major or Minor Key	Scale or Mode	Starting on...
Maj7♯5♯11	Any	Both	Lydian Augmented	The 9th of the chord

Lydian Augmented

Use a Lydian Augmented mode starting on the root of a Maj7♯5♯11 chord.

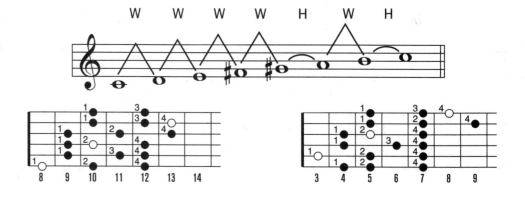

DOMINANT CHORDS
Unaltered

7, 9, 11, 13, and 7sus4 Chords

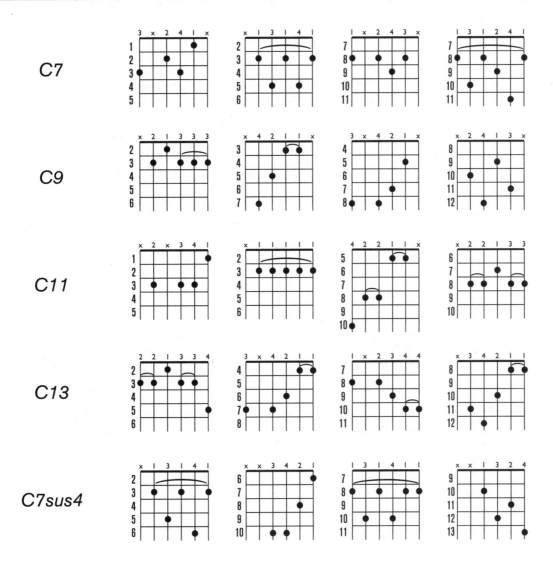

	C7
	C9
	C11
	C13
	C7sus4

Chord and Scale Chart

Chords	Function	Major or Minor Key	Scale or Mode	Starting on…
All unaltered dominant chords: 7, 9, 11, 13, and 7sus4 *except where marked **	Any	Major	Major Pentatonic	The root of the chord
	Any	Major	Major Pentatonic	The 4th of the chord
	Any	Major	Minor Pentatonic	The root of the chord
	Any	Major	Minor Pentatonic	The 5th of the chord
	Any	Major	Blues	The root of the chord
	Any	Major	Mixolydian	The root of the chord
	IV	Minor	Lydian ♭7*	The root of the chord
			*not good for 11 or 7sus4 chords	
	V	Minor	Mixolydian ♭6*	The root of the chord
			*not good for 13 chords	
	V	Minor	Phrygian Dominant*	The root of the chord
			*not good for 9 chords	
7sus4	Any	Both	Dorian	The root of the chord
	Any	Both	Dorian	The 5th of the chord

Major Pentatonic

Use a major pentatonic scale starting on the root of any dominant chord in a major key.

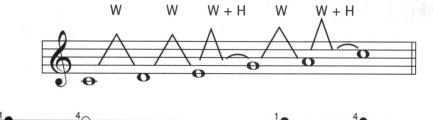

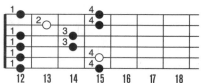

You can also use a major pentatonic scale starting on the 4th of any dominant chord in a major key.

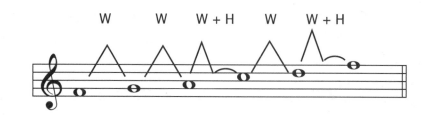

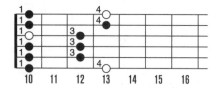

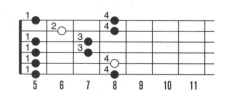

Minor Pentatonic

Use a minor pentatonic scale starting on the root of any dominant chord in a major key.

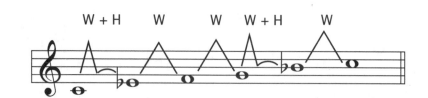

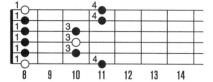

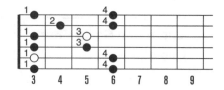

You can also use a minor pentatonic scale starting on the 5th of any dominant chord in a major key.

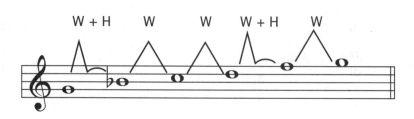

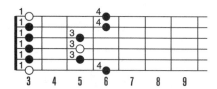

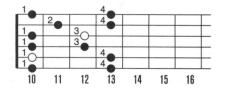

Blues Scale

Use a blues scale starting on the root of any dominant chord in a major key.

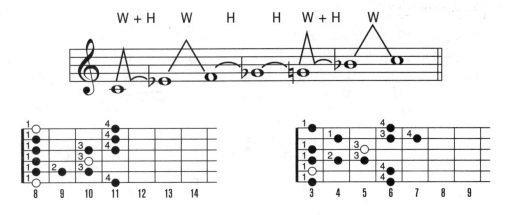

Mixolydian

Use the Mixolydian mode starting on the root of the chord.

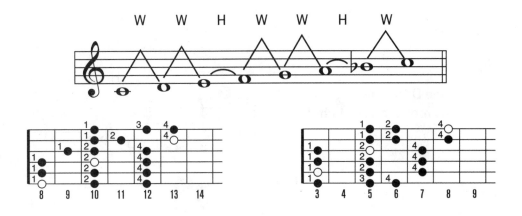

Lydian ♭7

Use the Lydian ♭7 mode starting on the root of any dominant chord other than an 11 chord.

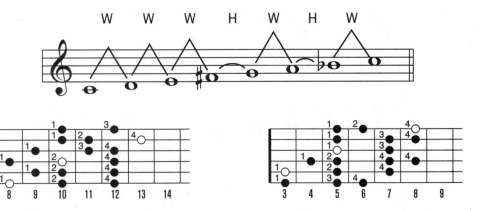

Mixolydian ♭6

Use the Mixolydian ♭6 mode starting on the root of any dominant chord other than a 13 chord.

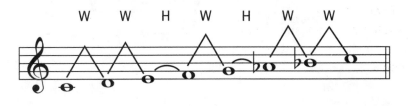

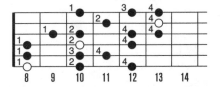

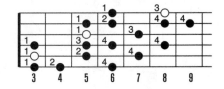

Phrygian Dominant

Use the Phrygian dominant mode starting on the root of any dominant chord, with the exception of 9 chords.

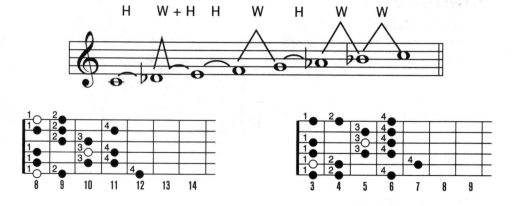

Dorian

Use the Dorian mode starting on the root of a 7sus4 chord.

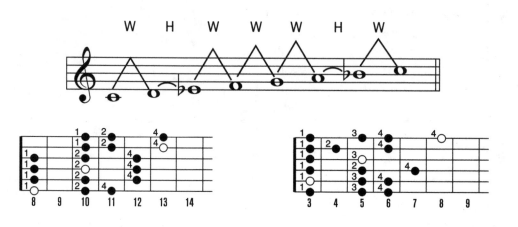

You can also use the Dorian mode starting from the 5th of a 7sus4 chord.

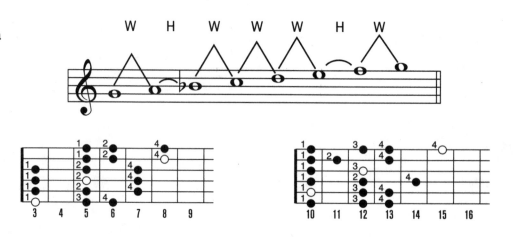

DOMINANT CHORDS
Altered

7♭5 Chords

C7♭5

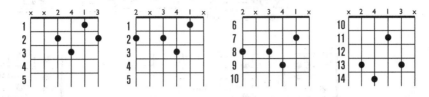

Chord and Scale Chart

Chords	Function	Major or Minor Key	Scale or Mode	Starting on…
	Any	Both	Whole Tone	The root of the chord
	Any	Both	Whole Tone	The 3rd of the chord
	Any	Both	Whole Tone	The ♭5 of the chord
7♭5	Any	Both	Whole Tone	The ♭7 of the chord
	Any	Both	Diminished	½ step above the root of the chord
	Any	Both	Lydian ♭7	The root of the chord
	Any	Both	Super Locrian	The root of the chord
	Any	Both	Blues	The root of the chord

Whole Tone

Use a whole tone scale from the root of a 7♭5 chord.

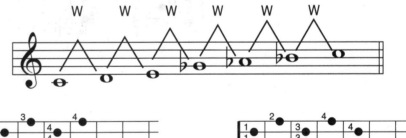

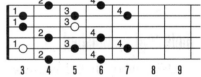

Use a whole tone scale from the 3rd of a 7♭5 chord.

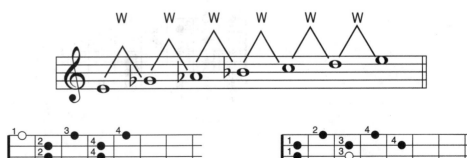

You can also use a whole tone scale starting on the ♭5 of a 7♭5 chord.

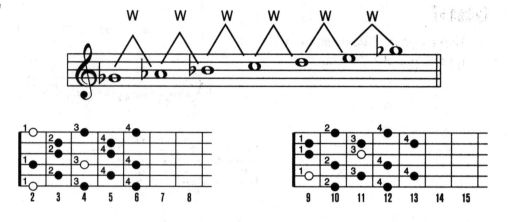

Or, you can use a whole tone scale starting on the ♭7 of a 7♭5 chord.

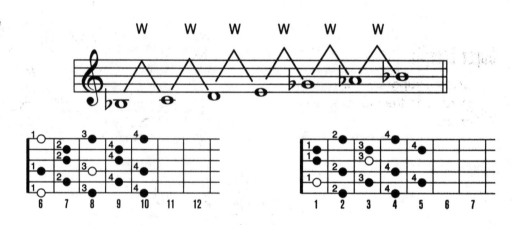

Whole-Half Diminished

Use a whole-half diminished scale starting one half step above the root of a 7♭5 chord.

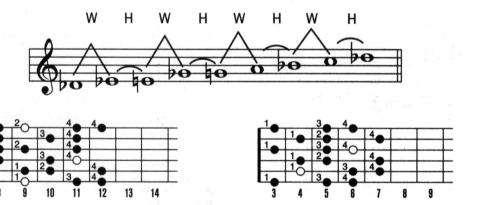

Lydian ♭7

Use a Lydian ♭7 scale starting on the root of a 7♭5 chord.

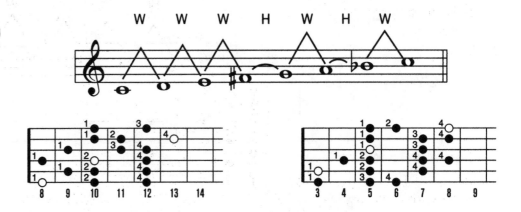

Super Locrian

Use the super Locrian mode starting on the root of a 7♭5 chord.

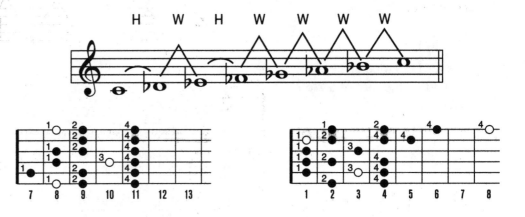

Blues

Use a blues scale starting on the root of a 7♭5 chord.

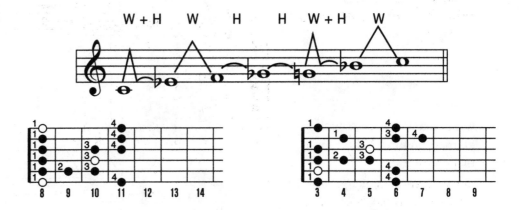

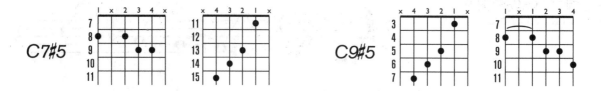

C7♯5   C9♯5

Chord and Scale Chart

Chords		Function	Major or Minor Key	Scale or Mode	Starting on...
7♯5 and 9♯5	{	Any	Both	Whole tone	The root of the chord
		Any	Both	Whole tone	The 3rd of the chord
		Any	Both	Whole tone	The ♯5 of the chord
		Any	Both	Whole tone	The ♭7 of the chord
		Any	Both	Mixolydian ♭6	The root of the chord
7♯5	{	Any	Both	Phrygian Dominant	The root of the chord
		Any	Both	Super Locrian	The root of the chord

Whole Tone

Use a whole tone scale starting on the root of a 7♯5 or 9♯5 chord.

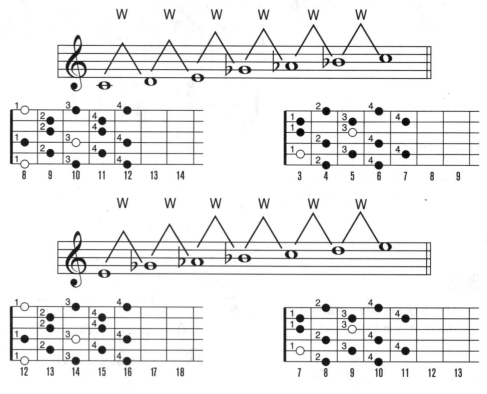

Or, use a whole tone scale starting on the ♯5 of a 7♯5 or 9♯5 chord.

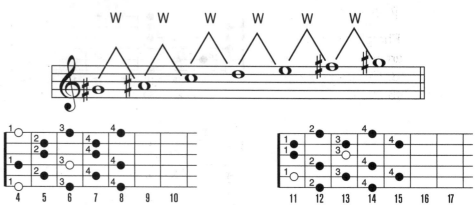

It is also possible to use a whole tone scale starting on the ♭7 of a 7♯5 or 9♯5 chord.

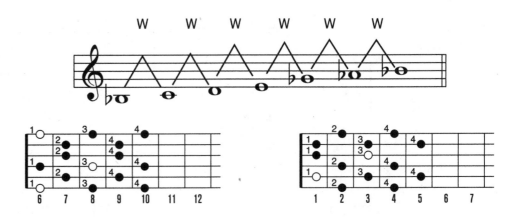

Super Locrian

Use the super Locrian mode starting on the root of a 7♯5 chord.

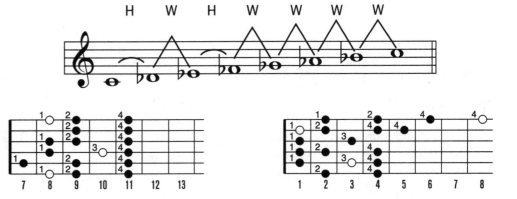

Mixolydian ♭6

Use the Mixolydian ♭6 mode starting on the root of a 7♯5 or 9♯5 chord.

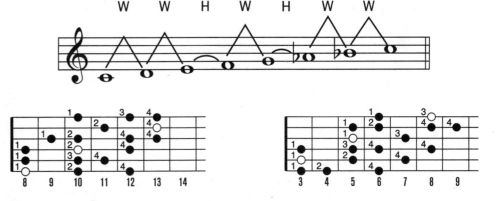

Phrygian Dominant

Use the Phrygian dominant mode starting on the root of a 7♯5 chord. This does not work for the 9♯5 chord.

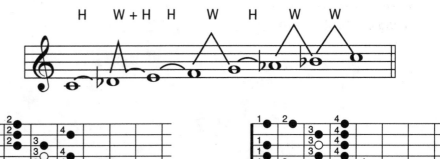

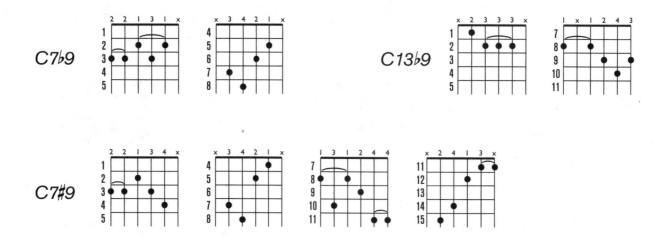

Chord and Scale Chart

Chords	Function	Major or Minor Key	Scale or Mode	Starting on...
7♭9, 13♭9, and 7♯9 (except where marked *)	Any	Both	Diminished	The 3rd of the chord
	Any	Both	Diminished	The 5th of the chord
	Any	Both	Diminished	The ♭7 of the chord
	Any	Both	Diminished	The ♭9 of the chord
	Any	Both	Diminished	½ step above the root of the chord
	Any	Both	Super Locrian	The root of the chord
	Any	Both	Phrygian Dominant*	The root of the chord

*not good for a 7♯9 chord

Chords	Function	Major or Minor Key	Scale or Mode	Starting on...
7♯9	Any	Both	Minor Pentatonic	The root of the chord
	Any	Both	Blues	The root of the chord
	Any	Both	Dorian	The root of the chord

Whole-Half Diminished

Use a whole-half diminished scale starting on the 3 of a 7♭9, 13♭9, or 7♯9 chord.

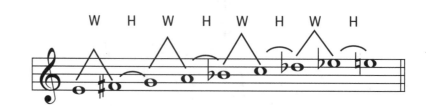

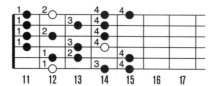

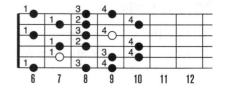

Use a diminished scale starting on the 5 of a 7♭9, 13♭9, or 7♯9 chord.

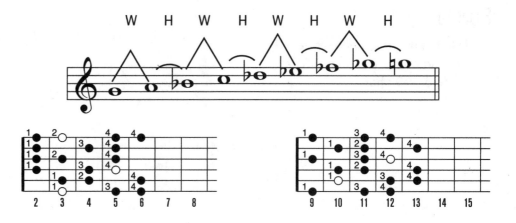

Use a diminished scale starting on the ♭7 of a 7♭9, 13♭9, or 7♯9 chord.

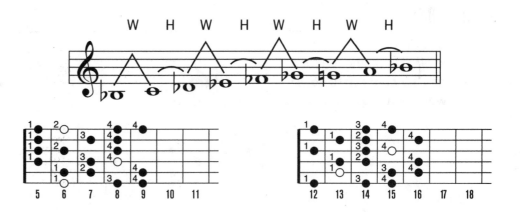

Use a diminished scale starting on the ♭9 or one half step above the root of a 7♭9, 13♭9, or 7♯9 chord.

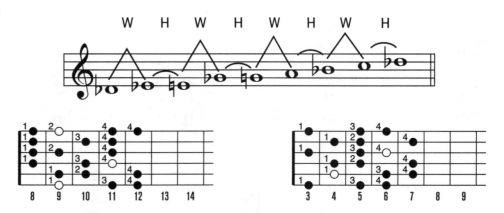

Super Locrian

Use the super Locrian mode starting on the root of a 7♭9, 13♭9, or 7♯9 chord.

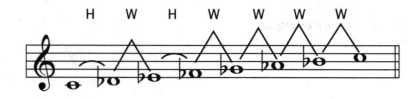

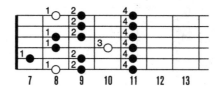
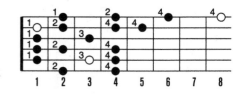

Phrygian Dominant

Use the Phrygian dominant mode starting on the root of a 7♭9 or 13♭9 chord. This does not work for a 7♯9 chord.

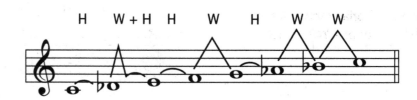

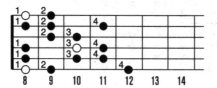
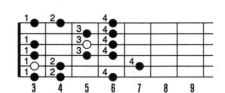

Minor Pentatonic

Use a minor pentatonic scale starting on the root of a 7♯9 chord.

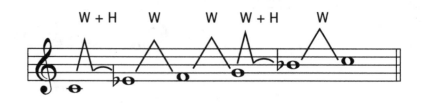

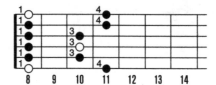
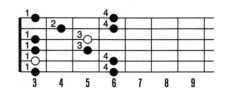

Blues

Use a blues scale starting on the root of a 7#9 chord.

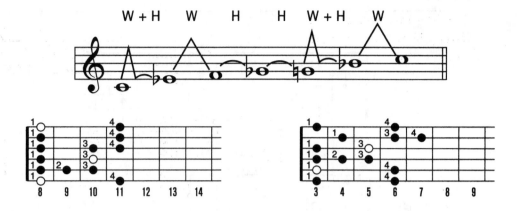

Dorian

Use the Dorian mode starting on the root of a 7#9 chord.

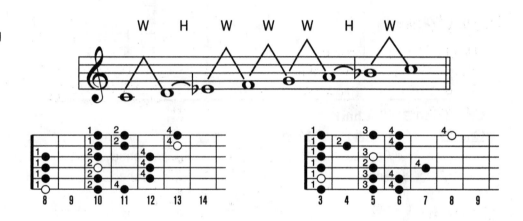

7♭5♭9, 7♭5#9, 13#9#11, and 7#5#9 Chords

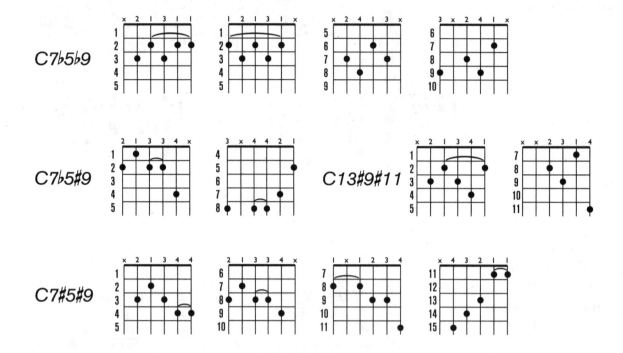

C7♭5♭9

C7♭5#9   C13#9#11

C7#5#9

Chord and Scale Chart

Chords	Function	Major or Minor Key	Scale or Mode	Starting on…
7♭5♭9, 7♭5#9, and 13#9#11	Any	Both	Diminished	Half step above the root of the chord
	Any	Both	Diminished	The 3 of the chord
	Any	Both	Diminished	The ♭7 of the chord
	Any	Both	Diminished	The ♭9 of the chord
	Any	Both	Super Locrian	The root of the chord
7♭5♭9	Any	Both	Major Pentatonic	Half step above the root of the chord
7♭5#9 and 13#9#11	Any	Both	Blues	The root of the chord
7#5#9	Any	Both	Super Locrian	The root of the chord

Whole-Half Diminished

Use a whole-half diminished scale starting on the 3 of a 7♭5♭9, 7♭5#9, or 13#9#11 chord.

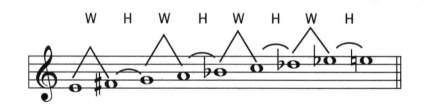

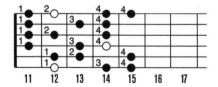

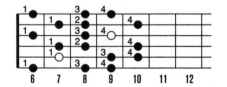

Use a diminished scale starting on the ♭7 of a 7♭5♭9, 7♭5♯9, or 13♯9♯11 chord.

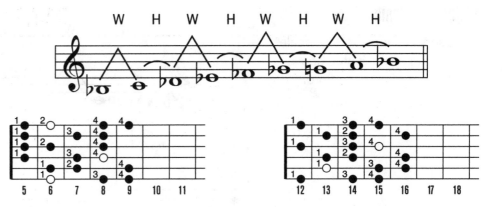

Use a diminished scale starting one half step above the root of a 7♭5♭9, 7♭5♯9, or 13♯9♯11 chord.

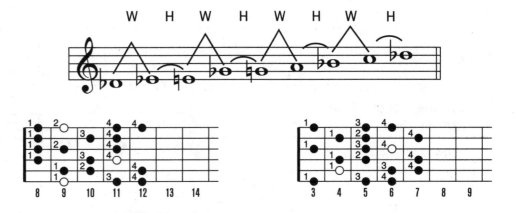

Super Locrian

Use the super Locrian mode starting on the root of a 7♭5♭9, 7♭5♯9, 13♯9♯11, or 7♯5♯9 chord.

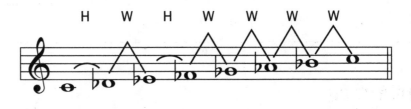

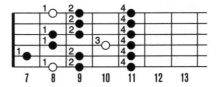

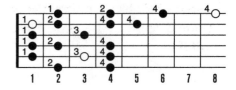

Major Pentatonic

Use a major pentatonic scale starting one half step above the root of a 7♭5♭9 chord.

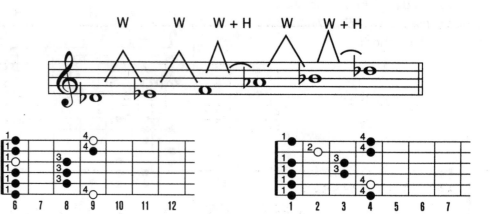

Blues

Use a blues scale starting from the root of a 7♭5♯9 or 13♯9♯11 chord.

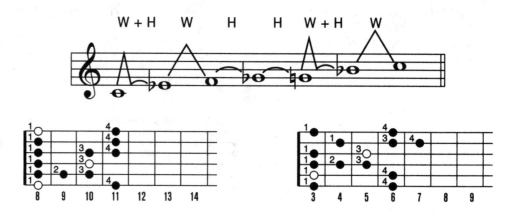

7#5♭9 Chords

C7#5♭9

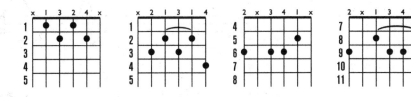

Chord and Scale Chart				
Chords	Function	Major or Minor Key	Scale or Mode	Starting on...
7#5♭9 {	Any.............Both.............Super Locrian..............The root of the chord			
	Any.............Both.............Phrygian Dominant........The root of the chord			

Super Locrian

Use the Phrygian dominant mode starting on the root of a 7#5♭9 chord.

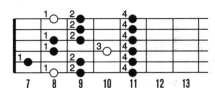

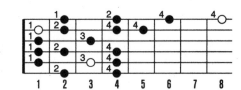

Phrygian Dominant

Use the Phrygian dominant mode starting on the root of a 7♭9 or 13♭9 chord. This does not work for a 7#9 chord.

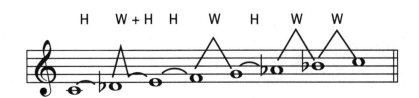

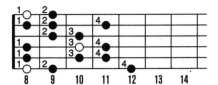

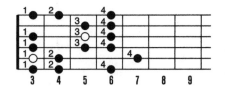

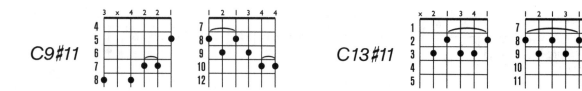

Chord and Scale Chart

Chords	Function	Major or Minor Key	Scale or Mode	Starting on...
9#11 and 13#11 { Any	Both		Lydian ♭7	The root of the chord
Any	Both		Blues	The root of the chord

Lydian ♭7

Use the Lydian ♭7 mode starting on the root of a 9#11 or 13#11 chord.

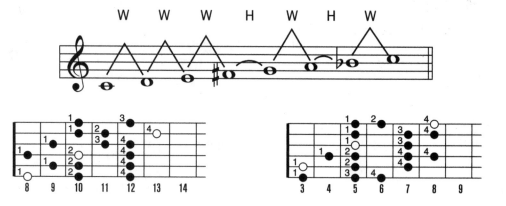

Blues

Use a blues scale starting on the root of a 9#11 or 13#11 chord.

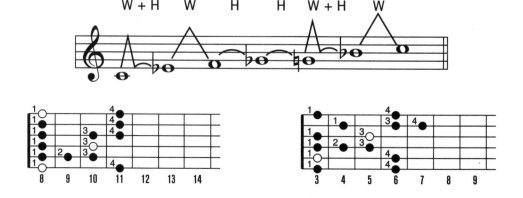

AUGMENTED TRIADS

CAug

Chord and Scale Chart

Chords	Function	Major or Minor Key	Scale or Mode	Starting on…
Aug {	Any	Both	Whole Tone	The root of the chord
	Any	Both	Whole Tone	The 3rd of the chord
	Any	Both	Whole Tone	The ♯5 of the chord

Whole Tone

Use a whole tone scale starting on the root of an augmented triad.

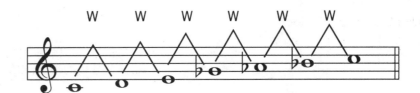

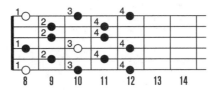 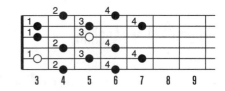

You can also use a whole tone scale starting on the 3rd of an augmented triad.

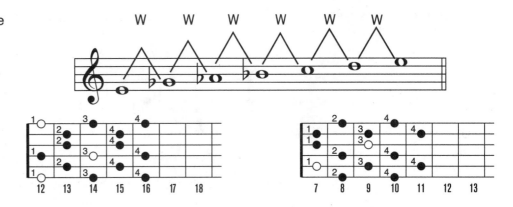

Use a whole tone scale starting on the ♯5 of an augmented triad.

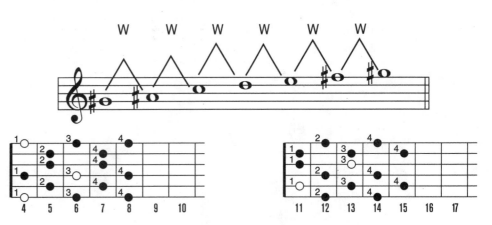

MINOR CHORDS

Cmin

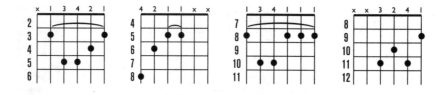

Chord and Scale Chart

Chords	Function	Major or Minor Key	Scale or Mode	Starting on...
Minor triads (min)	i	Minor	Natural Minor (Aeolian)	The root of the chord
	vi	Major		
	i	Minor	Harmonic Minor	The root of the chord
	i	Minor	Melodic Minor	The root of the chord
	i or ii	Minor	Minor Pentatonic	The root of the chord
	ii, iii, or vi	Major		
	ii	Major	Dorian	The root of the chord
	ii	Minor	Dorian ♭2	The root of the chord
	iii	Major	Phrygian	The root of the chord
	iv	Minor	Lydian ♭3♭7	The root of the chord

Natural Minor (Aeolian)

Use a natural minor scale starting on the root of a minor triad when it functions as i in a minor key or vi in a major key.

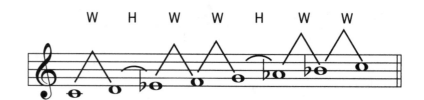

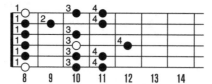

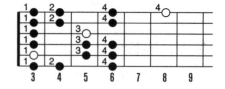

Harmonic Minor

Use a harmonic minor scale starting on the root of a minor triad when it functions as i in a minor key.

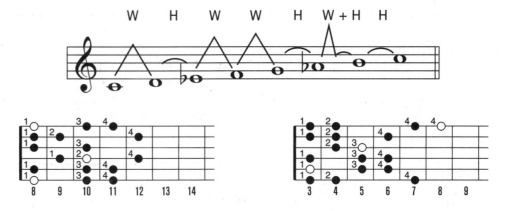

Melodic Minor

Use a melodic minor scale starting on the root of a minor triad when it functions as i in a minor key.

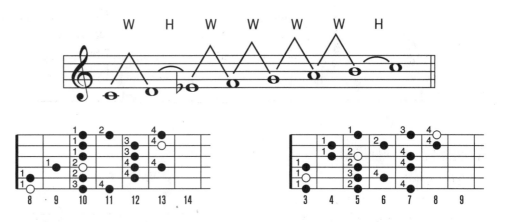

Minor Pentatonic

Use a minor pentatonic scale starting on the root of a minor triad when it functions as i or ii in a minor key; or when it functions as ii, iii, or vi in a major key.

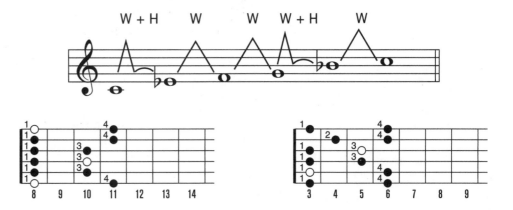

Dorian

Use the Dorian mode starting on the root of a minor triad when it functions as ii in a major key.

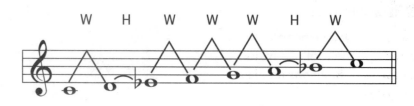

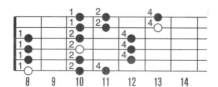 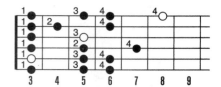

Dorian ♭2

Use the Dorian ♭2 mode starting on the root of a minor triad when it functions as ii in a minor key.

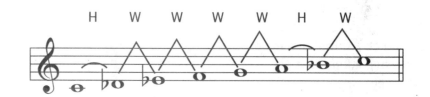

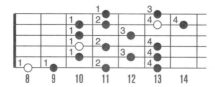 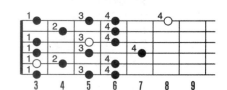

Phrygian

Use the Phrygian mode starting on the root of a minor triad when it functions as iii in a major key.

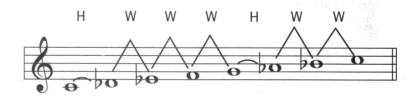

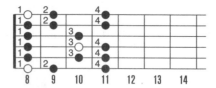 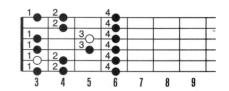

Lydian ♭3♭7

Use the Phrygian mode starting on the root of a minor triad when it functions as iii in a major key.

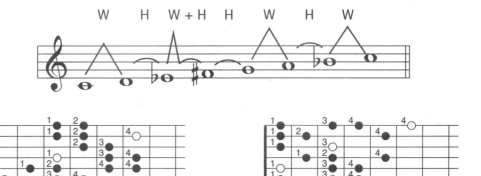

Jazz/rock fusion giant Al Di Meola developed his astonishing technique by spending several hours a day practicing scales with a metronome. In 1974, when he was only 19 years old, he joined Chick Corea's band Return to Forever, and has since made many solo recordings.

Cmin6

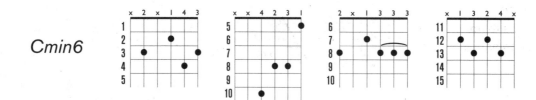

Chord and Scale Chart

Chord	Function	Major or Minor Key	Scale or Mode	Starting on…
min6	i, ii, iv	Minor	Minor Pentatonic	The root of the chord
	ii	Major		
	i	Minor	Melodic Minor	The root of the chord
	ii	Minor	Dorian ♭2	The root of the chord
	ii	Major	Dorian	The root of the chord
	iv	Minor	Lydian ♭3♭7	The root of the chord

Minor Pentatonic

Use a minor pentatonic scale starting on the root of a min6 chord when it functions as i, ii, or iv in a minor key, or when it functions as a ii in a major key.

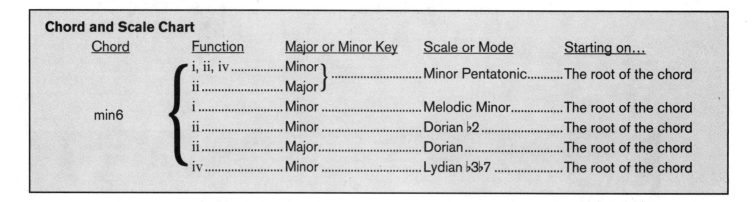

Melodic Minor

Use the melodic minor scale starting on the root of a min6 chord when it functions as i in a minor key.

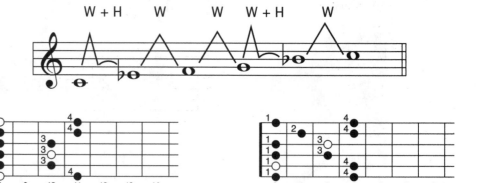
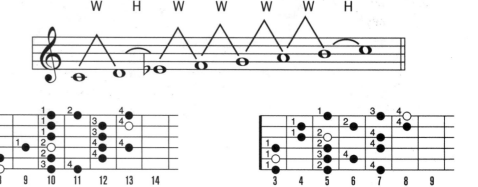

Dorian ♭2

Use the Dorian ♭2 mode starting on the root of a min6 chord when it functions as ii in a minor key.

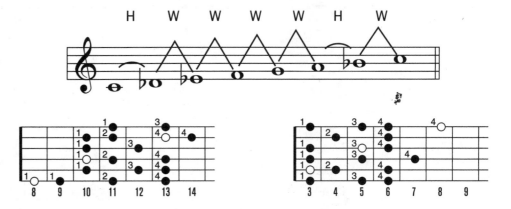

Dorian

Use the Dorian mode starting on the root of a min6 chord when it functions as ii in a major key.

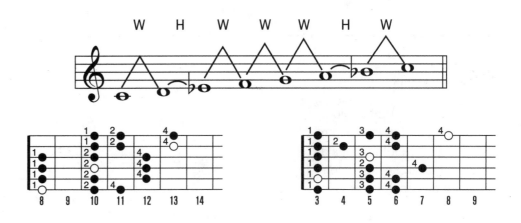

Lydian ♭3♭7

Use the Phrygian mode starting on the root of a minor triad when it functions as iii in a major key.

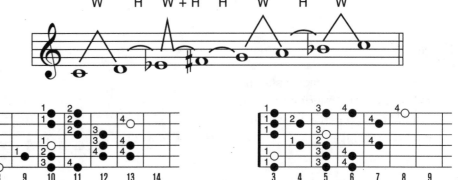

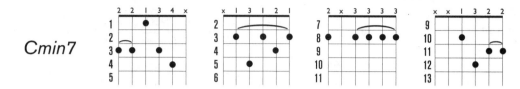

Cmin7

Chord and Scale Chart

Chords	Function	Major or Minor Key	Scale or Mode	Starting on...
	ii, iii, or vi	Major }	Minor Pentatonic	The root of the chord
	ii	Minor }		
min7	ii	Minor	Dorian ♭2	The root of the chord
	ii	Major	Dorian	The root of the chord
	iii	Major	Phrygian	The root of the chord
	iv	Minor	Lydian ♭3♭7	The root of the chord
	vi	Minor	Natural Minor (Aeolian)	The root of the chord

Minor Pentatonic

Use a minor pentatonic scale starting on the root of a min7 chord when it functions as ii in a minor key, or when it functions as ii, iii, or vi in major key.

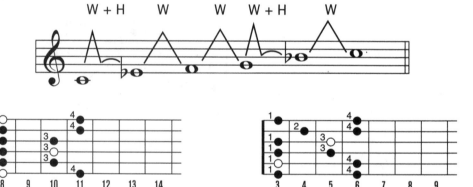

Dorian ♭2

Use the Dorian ♭2 mode starting on the root of a minor triad when it functions as ii in a minor key.

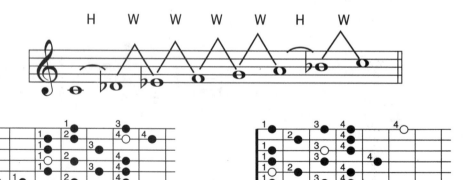

Dorian

Use the Dorian mode starting on the root of a min7 chord when it functions as ii in a major key.

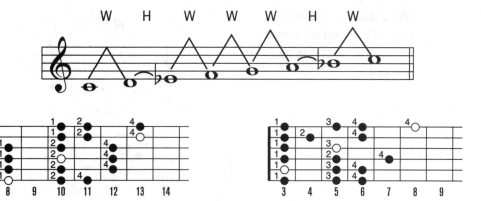

Phrygian

Use the Phrygian mode starting on the root of a min7 chord when it functions as iii in a major key.

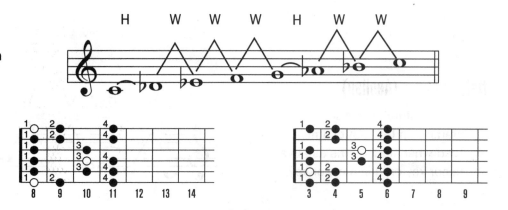

Buddy Guy (b. 1936) played on many famous recording sessions for Chess Records. Aside from his own successful performing and recording career, he has backed up the likes of Muddy Waters, Howlin' Wolf, and Little Walter.

Lydian ♭3♭7

Use the Lydian♭3♭7 mode starting on the root of a min7 chord when it functions as iv in a minor key.

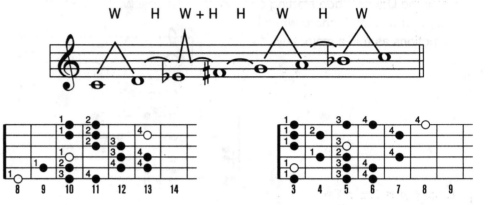

Natural Minor (Aeolian)

Use a natural minor scale starting on the root of a minor triad when it functions as i in a minor key or vi in a major key.

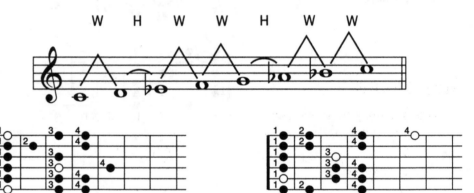

min9 Chords

Cmin9

 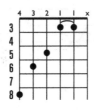 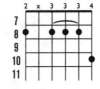

Chord and Scale Chart

Chords	Function	Major or Minor Key	Scale or Mode	Starting on...
min9	ii or vi	Major	Minor Pentatonic	The root of the chord
	ii	Major	Dorian	The root of the chord
	iv	Minor	Lydian ♭3♭7	The root of the chord
	vi	Major	Natural Minor (Aeolian)	The root of the chord

Minor Pentatonic

Use a minor pentatonic scale starting on the root of a min9 chord when it functions as ii or vi in a major key.

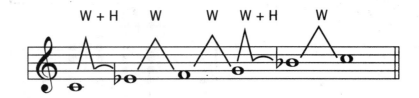

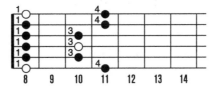   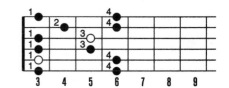

Dorian

Use the Dorian mode starting on the root of a min9 chord when it functions as ii in a major key.

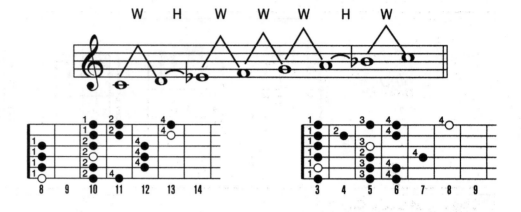

Lydian ♭3♭7

Use the Lydian ♭3♭7 mode starting on the root of a min9 when it functions as iv in a minor key.

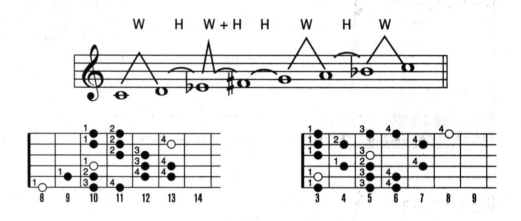

Natural Minor (Aeolian)

Use a natural minor scale (Aeolian mode) starting on the root of a min9 chord when it functions as vi in a major key.

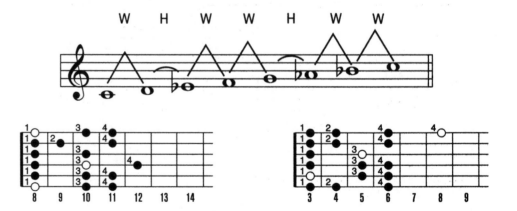

min11 Chords

Cmin11

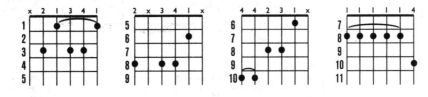

Chord and Scale Chart

Chords	Function	Major or Minor Key	Scale or Mode	Starting on...
min11	ii	Minor	Minor pentatonic	The root of the chord
	ii or iii	Major		
	ii	Major	Dorian	The root of the chord
	ii	Minor	Dorian ♭2* *when the 9th is not present	The root of the chord
	iii	Major	Phrygian* *when the 9th is not present	The root of the chord
	iv	Minor	Lydian♭3♭7	The root of the chord
	vi	Major	Natural Minor (Aeolian)	The root of the chord

Minor Pentatonic

Use a minor pentatonic scale starting on the root of a min11 chord when it functions as ii in a minor key, or ii or iii in a major key.

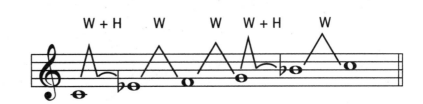

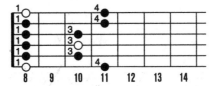

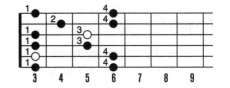

Dorian

Use the Dorian mode starting on the root of a min11 chord when it functions as ii in a major key.

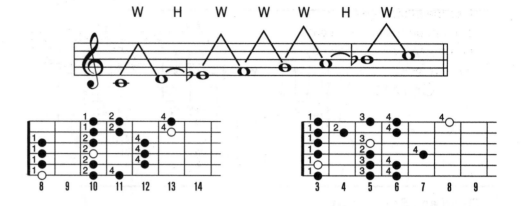

Dorian ♭2

Use the Dorian ♭2 mode starting on the root of a min11 chord when the 9th is not present and it functions as ii in a minor key

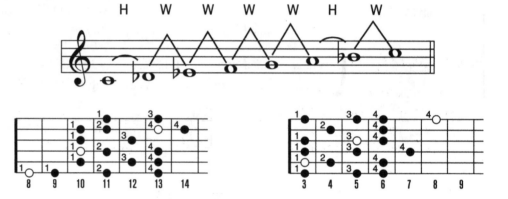

Phrygian

Use the Phrygian mode starting on the root of a min7 chord when it functions as iii in a major key.

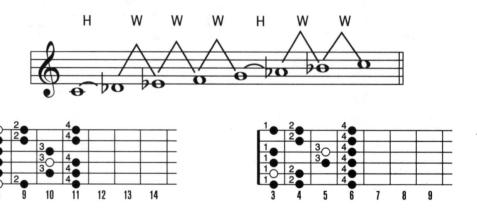

Lydian ♭3♭7

Use the Lydian ♭3♭7 mode starting on the root of a min11 chord when it functions as iv in a minor key.

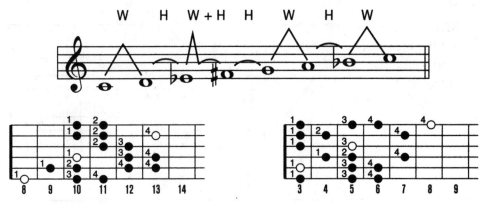

Natural Minor (Aeolian)

Use a natural minor scale (Aeolian mode) starting on the root of a min11 chord when it functions as vi in a major key.

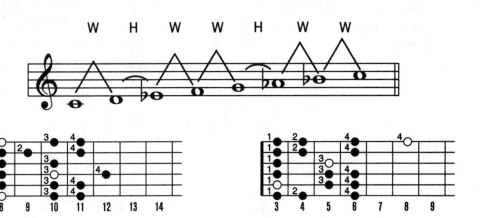

Cmin13

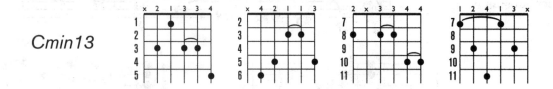

Chord and Scale Chart

Chords	Function	Major or Minor Key	Scale or Mode	Starting on…
	ii	Minor	Minor pentatonic	The root of the chord
	ii or iii	Major		
	ii	Major	Dorian	The root of the chord
min11	ii	Minor	Dorian ♭2*	The root of the chord
			*when the 9th is not present	
	iii	Major	Phrygian*	The root of the chord
			*when the 9th is not present	
	iv	Minor	Lydian♭3♭7	The root of the chord
	vi	Major	Natural Minor (Aeolian)	The root of the chord

Minor Pentatonic

Use a minor pentatonic scale starting on the root of a min13 chord when it functions as ii in a minor key, or ii or iii in a major key.

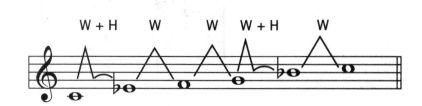

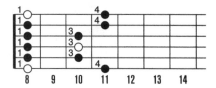

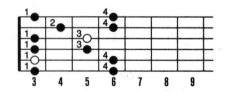

Dorian

Use the Dorian mode starting on the root of a min13 chord when it functions as ii in a major key.

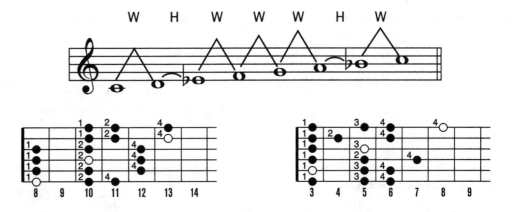

Dorian ♭2

Use the Dorian ♭2 mode starting on the root of a min13 chord when the 9th is not present and it functions as ii in a minor key.

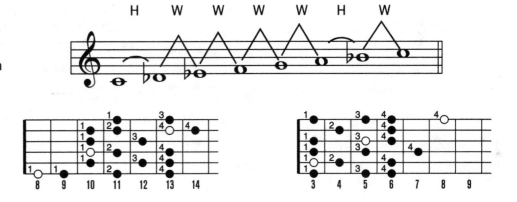

Lydian ♭3♭7

Use the Lydian ♭3♭7 mode starting on the root of a min13 chord when it functions as iv in a minor key.

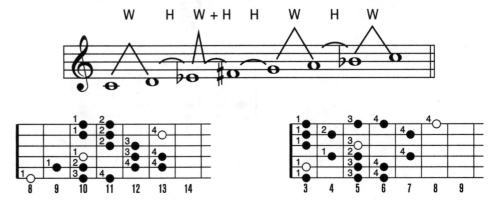

Cmin(maj7)

Chord and Scale Chart

Chords	Function	Major or Minor Key	Scale or Mode	Starting on...
Cmin(Maj7) {	Any	Both	Harmonic Minor	The root of the chord
	Any	Both	Melodic Minor	The root of the chord

Harmonic Minor

Use a harmonic minor scale starting on the root of a min(Maj7) chord.

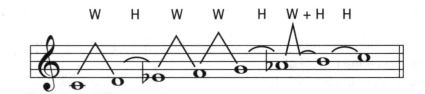

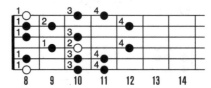   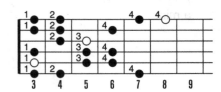

Melodic Minor

Use a melodic minor scale starting on the root of a min(Maj7) chord.

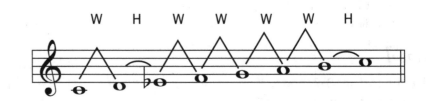

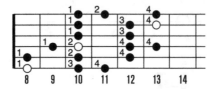   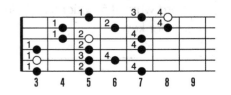

DIMINISHED CHORDS

dim, dim7, and
min7♭5 (half-diminished) Chords

Cdim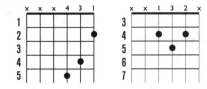

Cdim7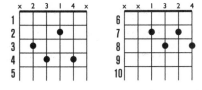

Cmin7♭5

Chord and Scale Chart

Chords	Function	Major or Minor Key	Scale or Mode	Starting on...
Diminished triads (dim) and dim7 chords	Any	Both	Diminished	The root of the chord
	Any	Both	Diminished	The ♭3 of the chord
	Any	Both	Diminished	The ♭5 of the chord
	Any	Both	Diminished	The ♭♭7 of the chord
	Any	Both	7th Mode Harmonic Minor	The root of the chord
min7♭5 (half-diminished)	vii	Major	Locrian	The root of the chord
	ii	Minor	Locrian #6	The root of the chord
	vi	Minor	Locrian #2	The root of the chord
	vii	Minor	Super Locrian	The root of the chord

♭♭ = Double flat. Lower
the note by one
whole step (two
half steps).

Whole-Half Diminished

Use a diminished scale starting on the root of a diminished triad or a dim7 chord.

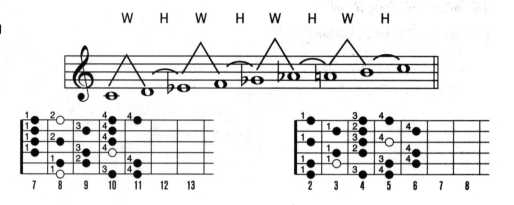

Use a diminished scale starting on the ♭3 of a diminished triad or a dim7 chord.

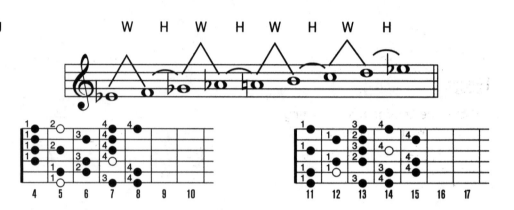

Use a diminished scale starting on the ♭5 of a diminished triad or a dim7 chord.

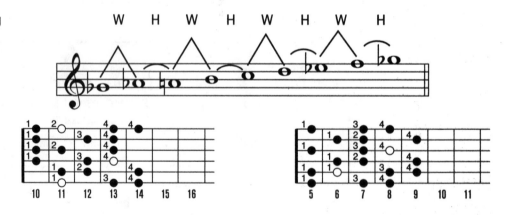

Use a diminished scale starting on the ♭♭7 of a diminished triad or a dim7 chord.

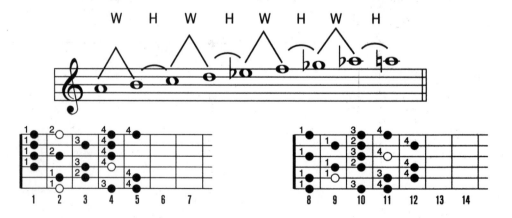

7th Mode Harmonic Minor

Use the 7th mode of the harmonic minor scale starting on the root of a diminished triad or a dim7 chord.

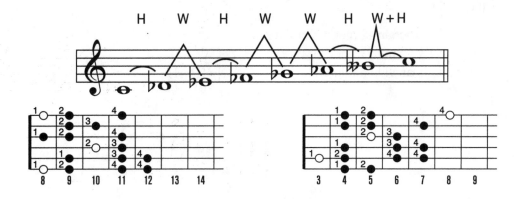

Locrian

Use the Locrian mode starting on the root of a min7b5 chord when it functions as vii in a major key.

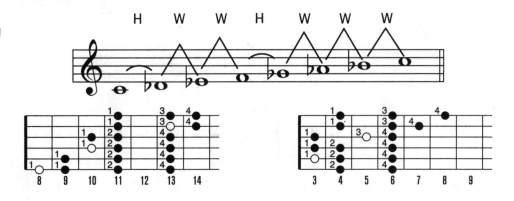

Locrian #6

Use the Locrian #6 mode starting on the root of a min7b5 chord when it functions as ii in a minor key.

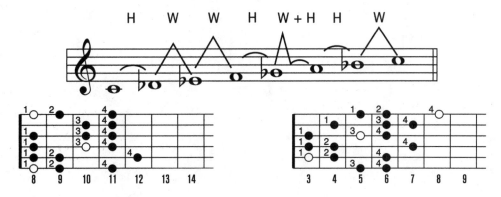

Locrian #2

Use the Locrian #2 mode starting on the root of a min7♭5 chord when it functions as vi in a minor key.

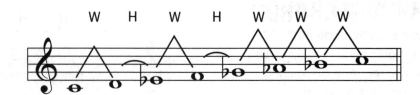

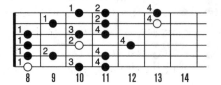

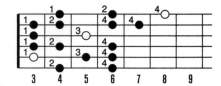

Super Locrian

Use the Phrygian dominant mode starting on the root of a 7#5♭9 chord.

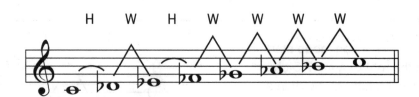

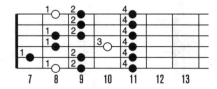

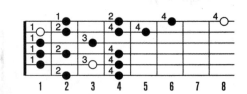

QUARTAL-3 CHORDS

In conventional harmony, we use chords that are constructed primarily from stacking 3rds. In quartal harmony, chords are constructed by stacking 4ths.

Chords built with 4ths have a sort of rootless character, making them rather ambiguous in regard to key centers. They have no standardized names so we will name them with the lowest note of the chord. If the bass is C, and there are a total of three notes a 4th apart, we will call the chord "C quartal-3." If there are four notes in the stack, we will call it "C quartal-4," and so on. Quartal chords can be used to harmonize melodies which would ordinarily be harmonized with a minor chord.

C Quartal-3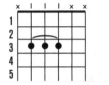

Chord and Scale Chart

Chords	Function	Major or Minor Key	Scale or Mode	Starting on…
Quartal-3	Any	Both	Minor Pentatonic	The root of the chord
	Any	Both	Minor Pentatonic	The 4th of the chord
	Any	Both	Minor Pentatonic	The ♭7 of the chord
	Any	Both	Dorian	The root of the chord
	Any	Both	Dorian	The 4th of the chord
	Any	Both	Dorian	The ♭7 of the chord

Minor Pentatonic

Use a minor pentatonic scale starting on the root of a min13 chord when it functions as ii in a minor key, or ii or iii in a major key.

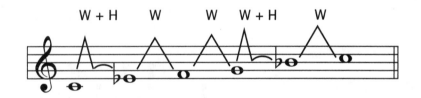

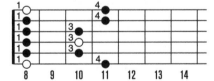 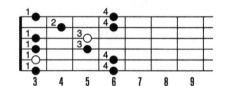

You can also use a minor pentatonic scale starting on the 4th of a quartal-3 chord.

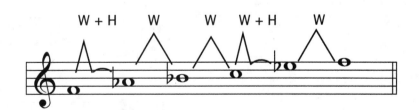

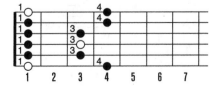 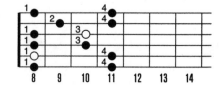

Or, use the minor pentatonic
scale starting from the ♭7 of a
quartal-3 chord.

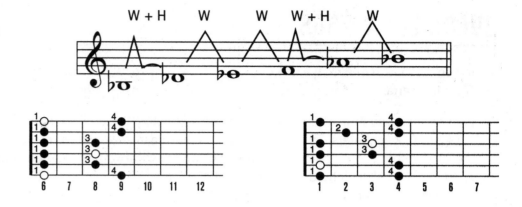

Dorian

Use the Dorian mode starting
from the root of a quartal-3
chord.

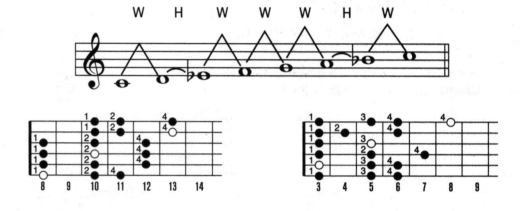

You can also use the Dorian
mode starting from the 4th of a
quartal-3 chord.

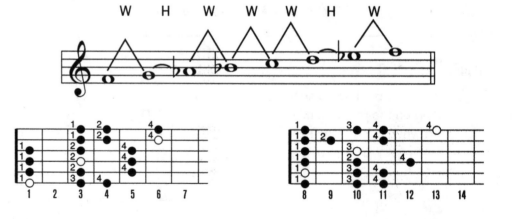

Or, you can use the Dorian
mode starting on the ♭7 of a
quartal-3 chord.

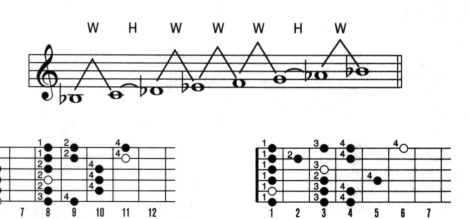